DON'T REMEMBER

RICH SILVERS

Books by Rich Silvers

HAVE YOU SEEN HER?

DON'T REMEMBER

SUM LIVES (FORTHCOMING)

DON'T REMEMBER

A NOVEL

RICH SILVERS

Conure Press

Don't Remember
Rich Silvers

Conure Press
145 Hitching Post Lane
Yorktown Heights, N.Y. 10598
conurepress@verizon.net

For more information about this book, visit www.richsilvers.com

Edition ISBNs
Trade Paperback 978-0-9854944-3-8
E-book 978-0-9854944-2-1

First Edition 2016

This edition was prepared for printing by The Editorial Department
7650 E. Broadway, #308, Tucson, Arizona 85710
www.editorialdepartment.com

Cover design by Pete Garceau
Book design by Morgana Gallaway

For Cathy

ACKNOWLEDGEMENTS

Thanks, Mom, for your wisdom and grace. It continues to inspire me.

My wife, Cathy, continues to support and believe in me. Hon, I wouldn't be this far without you.

Renni Browne's wisdom and Shannon Roberts' plotting prowess guided me through the developmental and line-editing processes. This book wouldn't exist without them. You two truly are the A-Team!

Beth Jusino wrote compelling copy. Jane Ryder always stepped in at just the right moment to make things happen. Morgana Gallaway did the slick interior design, and Doug Wagner copy-edited with a fine eye for detail. Pete Garceau, your cool covers always manage to capture the essence of the story.

Any mistakes are mine.

Dad, I know you're up there still watching, working your magic . . .

CHAPTER 1

Julian made bets with fate.

Like his tank would fill before the next car pulled into the gas station. He'd reach the cashier before the tall man in the other line. If the balled-up crumpled paper landed in the wastebasket, he'd get promoted.

And now?

If he got through the intersection without stopping, he wouldn't lose Julia.

He accelerated down Wendt toward Brewster. The road that cut through the small upstate town was steep. Speedometer up to thirty-five. Steady. The intersection was fifty yards away. Would the light be green when he got there?

He saw Julia's thick black hair falling down her back as she screamed an obscenity.

She loved to be touched. He loved to touch her. As she'd

lay on the bed, he'd trace his fingers down her spine and time would fall away. "Don't stop," she'd moan. He wouldn't.

Thirty yards.

His speedometer was at thirty-five. Ten yards.

He looked up at the light and kept going.

CHAPTER 2

*P*ain on the left side of his body, like he'd been burned. Had he? His left leg was raised. Metal taste in his mouth.

How'd I get here?

Julian was in a white room. Julia stood over him. A fluorescent light was over her shoulder. She was beautiful: full lips, high cheeks, ice blue eyes.

"Julian." Her face was creased.

He couldn't speak. He touched his jaw—something metallic was in his mouth. His left leg was in a cast and he had a searing sensation with each breath.

"It'll take a while, but everything's going to be fine." She sounded confident as her fingers combed his hair, her cool touch more soothing than her words. "You're going to be fine."

He knew he was in a hospital, but he didn't know how he'd gotten there.

"You were in a bad car accident, hon," Julia said. "A doctor from this hospital broadsided you."

He tried putting the pieces together, but he couldn't find them—a hole in his memory. His eyes felt heavy. He was ready to let go, at least for a while.

"Yes, that's it." Julia's gentle yet firm voice led him to sleep. "Rest."

———

He dreamed he was driving a monster truck. His feet pressed both brakes to the metal. Neither worked. No steering wheel, hands tied behind his back. "*Julia!*" he yelled, going down a waterfall. Stones pelted his windshield and webs of cracked glass spread out before him. His speedometer spun round and round, first one way, then the other. Water smashed the truck. The compartment flooded. He couldn't breathe.

He woke with a start. No one was in the room with him. *Where'd she go?*

His eyes slid right. The windows lining the side of the room were black. Had it been dark when Julia was here?

A young nurse walked into the room. She was pretty with dirty blond hair. He'd never seen her before. She smiled. A man in a white lab coat was next to her.

"Mr. Barnes, I'm Dr. Stephan Halay. I hope you're feeling better."

His mouth was still wired shut. He was thirsty.

"Do you recall your automobile accident?" Halay said. "Blink once for 'yes' and twice for 'no.'"

He tried to remember. He couldn't.

He blinked twice.

The doctor turned toward the nurse. She looked serious.

Julian's stomach tumbled. A part of his life had been erased. He felt dumb, like the day he got a forty-five on the Trig Regents.

"Do you know your name is Julian Barnes?" Dr. Halay leaned closer.

He blinked once.

The doctor looked pleased and the nurse sighed with relief.

"You're young." Halay picked up his chart. He flipped a page on it and then back again. "You'll heal quickly." He took a thin flashlight out of his breast pocket, pushed up Julian's eyelid, and shone the light in his left eye, then his right. "You'll be here for a few more days and you'll wear this for three months." He tapped the cast with the flashlight. Julian didn't feel a thing. "You'll also be on a liquid diet for a month." He ticked off his fingers. "You have a broken leg, fractured jaw, and two cracked ribs."

Julian noticed a whiteboard on the table next to his bed. He pointed to it. The nurse handed it to him along with a black marker.

WHY CAN'T I REMEMBER?

"The accident could've been especially traumatic for you in some way," the doctor said. "In any case, amnesia is not uncommon in such situations. It's more often temporary than not. Do you recall getting into your car yesterday?"

YES.

"It's good you remember that."

He was on his way to Julia's apartment. He wanted to surprise her with orchestra seats to *Phantom of the Opera*. He hoped Andrew Lloyd Weber and the saltimbocca at Cara Mia would help get things back on track, the way they were in the beginning.

Where are those tickets now?

"When were you born?" Halay said.

7/11/77.

"Excellent." Dr. Halay looked over the top of his reading glasses. "Give it some time. Don't force it. The rest will come, though it's hard to say how long that will be."

"My name is Leah." The nurse tucked in the blanket on his bed. "I'm here Tuesday to Saturday, four to twelve. If you need anything, push this call button." She handed it to him.

"I'll give you something for the pain," Halay said. "We can be liberal with it the first week. But after that we're going to have to scale back. We don't want you addicted, right?"

Julian nodded. He wasn't into drugs.

You're addicted to Julia.

"You'll live." Halay patted Julian's shoulder. "Now if you don't have any more questions, I've got to check on another patient."

He had plenty of questions. But none of them were for the doctor.

CHAPTER 3

Julian dreamed he and Julia were in the front row of a movie theater. Gigantic images of men running came at them. He had his arm around her. She wore sunglasses. He kissed her and she crumbled—gone. Where was she? He ran down a beach, screaming her name. The sun burned his back. He looked under the seat. Julia laughed.

He drifted toward consciousness and slowly opened his eyes.

An extremely attractive woman sat in the club chair at the foot of his bed. She had short blond hair and blue eyes. Probably early thirties, wearing a dark skirt, a white blouse, and a pearl necklace.

"Mr. Barnes," she said, "I'm Evelyn Wright, Dr. Alan Wright's sister." She paused. "The man who supposedly ran into you?"

Julian swallowed hard. His throat was scratchy. He reached for the cup and sipped some water.

"Are you in a lot of pain?" she said.

He nodded.

"I'm sorry to hear that." Her hands were folded in her lap. "But the fact remains Alan has saved hundreds of lives, and if he continues to operate, he'll save hundreds more."

WHY ISN'T HE HERE?

She looked at her watch.

"He will be in a few minutes." She rose and stepped closer to the bed. "I wanted to talk to you first . . . give you the proper perspective."

I DON'T REMEMBER WHAT HAPPENED.

"That's what we heard." She ran her finger along the metal bar on the side of his bed. "And the witness . . ."

THERE WAS A WITNESS?

"Yes, but things aren't as cut and dried as they seem, Mr. Barnes."

WAS YOUR BROTHER DRINKING?

"No." She stepped back, looking like she'd just swallowed something bitter. "He was coming from the hospital. Imagine the discipline and concentration needed to operate on brains. He's literally performed miracles."

WAS HE TIRED?

"Mr. Barnes, Alan has incredible stamina. He's amazing. If he wasn't my brother, I'd marry him."

TELL ME ABOUT THE ACCIDENT.

"Alan swears the light was green. Not yellow or red or anything in between—green. He wasn't speeding, wasn't distracted. Not drunk, texting, or falling asleep. He was just taking a friend home because she was inebriated. One more good deed after a day of them. Then *bam*." She smacked her hands together so hard he flinched. "Your car is there. He had no chance to stop. None whatsoever."

Remember—

He is walking toward Julia's apartment. He comes to her car, puts his hand on the hood. It's warm. She worked late? He makes his way toward the entrance. A man with a little dog opens the door. Julian goes inside. The elevator isn't there. He takes the stairs, two at a time . . . Nothing after that.

WHAT DO YOU WANT FROM ME?

"Admit you're at fault."

I CAN'T—UNTIL I KNOW I AM.

"That's not going to work." She was staring at him, making him uncomfortable.

WHY DON'T YOU BELIEVE WITNESS?

"He's mistaken or a liar. The point is, Alan can't be incarcerated."

A man in a wheelchair entered. He had on a robe and pajamas. He was handsome, early forties with short dark hair. A buxom woman in a white uniform came in behind him. When he turned toward the nurse and whispered in her ear, she departed.

"Mr. Barnes, my name is Dr. Alan Wright." He rolled his wheelchair closer. He covered his mouth as he gazed at Julian. "I'm so sorry, I . . ."

"Alan." Evelyn quickly moved around the bed to Wright's side.

"Eve, we were waiting for you," Wright whispered.

"Mr. Barnes and I were having a nice chat. Weren't we?" Julian nodded.

Wright had probably always been the hero, the savior. Now he was accused of causing another's pain. He pictured Evelyn Wright, with her pretty, determined face, telling her brother to *fight the good fight.*

"I know you can't talk." Wright's fingers were long and slender. It was easy to imagine them holding a scalpel, performing an intricate procedure. "I'm sure my light was green." He held Julian's stare. "I know the witness says otherwise."

Evelyn laid a hand on Wright's shoulder.

"I'm a very attentive driver," he said.

Julian picked up the whiteboard.

I DON'T REMEMBER.

"I've heard." Wright's voice was raspy. "I didn't run the light, but I want to help you."

"Alan." Evelyn knelt next to him. "Are you certain you want to do this? It may not bode well for proving your innocence."

"Eve, whatever else happened, my car ran into his. He could be affected by his injuries for the rest of his life and I'm in a position to ease his burden." Wright looked at him. "I'd like to offer you a million dollars."

Julian made seventy-five thousand dollars a year as an internal auditor. His goal was to amass a million by forty. But when he'd turned thirty-four last April, he had only a quarter of that.

UNCONDITIONALLY?

"One stipulation: you and I will have nothing to do with

this matter ever again. You're not to speak of it unless required by law. Is that something you can agree to?"

YES.

"Do you have a lawyer?" Wright said.

NO.

"Get one who's flexible." Evelyn had her hands on her hips. "If we're going to do this, let's do it quickly." She shook her head. "This is a mistake, giving him money. If it's about Cheryl—"

"It's about doing the right thing when one is in a position to."

"You help a lot of people. You don't need to help him." Evelyn pointed to Julian. "He's the one who caused the accident."

"Eve, that's enough," Wright whispered. "Not here."

"Fine." Evelyn gazed at Julian. "Once you have representation, we can proceed with the settlement. Hopefully, your attorney will work with us to expedite it." She turned to Wright. "Better?"

"Eve, I thought we talked about this."

"And I thought you didn't want to talk here."

Alan sighed and pressed his fingertips to his temples.

The buxom nurse reappeared, but Evelyn held up a hand.

"It's all right, Delores. I'll bring my brother back to his room."

The nurse's nostrils flared, and then she turned and left.

"Come on, Alan." Evelyn grabbed the handles of his wheelchair. "We're done here."

Julian felt a surge of relief as she pushed her brother out the door.

CHAPTER 4

"Mr. Barnes." A man in a gray double-breasted suit stood alongside Julian's bed. He was tan, trim, with long silver hair combed straight back. He had to be in his sixties. "I'm Milton Zorn. It's a pleasure to meet you."

He stuck out his hand. Julian shook it. Zorn had a huge sapphire pinky ring, wore designer cologne, and had a firm grip.

"Your fiancée left a message with my secretary." Zorn rose up on the balls of his feet, hands behind his back. "I have another client in the hospital, so I figured I'd stop by."

Which sounded fine—except that he and Julia weren't engaged, and Julia would never call a lawyer without consulting with him first.

"There are some forms you'll have to sign." The attorney snapped open a slim attaché. "I have them right here." He held up a stack of papers as if it were Exhibit A.

WHY DO I NEED YOU?

"You still don't remember your accident?"

He shook his head.

"That proves the extent of the trauma." Zorn raised a finger and started pacing. Julian found it easy to imagine this man in a courtroom, giving his summation, knowing what to say to get the jury to rule in his client's favor. "All I need is your signature." He gave Julian a pen and the stack of papers held together by a big black binder clip.

Julian started reading.

"Most of it is boilerplate." Zorn hooked his thumbs under his red suspenders. "Things in there for your protection as well as mine. Nothing to be concerned with."

The words were blurry as he reread the same sentences: Julian Barnes herein referred to as Client engages the services of Milton S. Zorn Esquire. Client agrees to terms and conditions set forth below . . .

"You were hit by Dr. Alan Wright Jr.," Zorn said. "An eyewitness says Wright ran the light. You're lucky your injuries aren't life-threatening. Unfortunately, I can't say the same about the doctor's passenger."

Julian's stomach shook. A PASSENGER?

"Cheryl Star. A nurse at the hospital. She and Wright were an item. Pretty serious, as I hear it."

SHE DIED?

"Yes. Wright could be tried for vehicular manslaughter, probably in the second degree."

SO HE COULD GO TO PRISON? Now Evelyn's insistence, her aggression, made sense.

"The district attorney is still gathering evidence, but yes, if they decide to press charges and if Dr. Wright gets convicted, he could. You have serious injuries. They'll want a nondisclosure—that's standard." The attorney looked him up and down. "We'll ask for two and won't take less than a million."

He wouldn't tell Zorn about Wright's offer, at least not yet.

WHO IS THIS WITNESS?

"Neal Store." Zorn pointed. "Once you sign those papers, I can find out more."

Zorn seemed on the level—though how he got here wasn't.

NEED TIME TO THINK.

"I represented another client in a suit against the Wrights." Zorn spoke lower. "We negotiated a fair settlement, and I expect the same in your situation. I've been at this for thirty-five years. What do you say?"

Evelyn made it clear Julian's attorney should be *flexible*. Could she have sent Zorn because of their prior dealings?

WILL CALL YOU TOMORROW.

"As I said, your fiancée asked me to come." Zorn checked his fingernails.

NEED TO SLEEP ON IT.

"That's fair." Zorn returned the papers to his briefcase and shut it. "Fortuitously, there's a lull in my caseload." He reached into his wallet and dealt a business card onto the table next to Julian's bed. "Retain me. You won't regret it." He turned and left.

Julian had no interest in a lawsuit. Alan Wright seemed like a decent man, and his offer of a million dollars seemed fair.

Even if Evelyn had called Zorn, Julian saw no reason not to use him. The attorney seemed like someone who would expedite things. The less conflict the sooner the Wright siblings would be out of his life.

CHAPTER 5

Julian woke with a queasy stomach and a stiff neck. He turned his head to loosen it. Leah sat in a chair next to his bed, her hands cupped in her lap.

He tried to speak. A mumble was all he could muster. His face felt warm.

"Are you okay?" Leah's eyebrows knitted together.

He nodded but wasn't so sure. His chest was sweaty, his back was clammy, and he was frightened for the first time. This was serious. The doctor said he'd heal, but it wouldn't be easy. His body was working overtime to rejuvenate itself, pulling in all its resources like an army under attack. He was mortal—something he didn't usually think about. His injuries were a forceful reminder.

"It'll take time." Leah touched his shoulder. "But you *will* feel like yourself again."

That was all he wanted.

A man in a brown uniform stood just outside the doorway. He had a buffing machine with him.

"Hi, Melvin," Leah said.

"Mind if I do the floor?" Melvin looked around. "It won't take long."

"You okay with that?" Leah put her hand on top of Julian's.

He nodded—he could use the distraction.

Melvin started up the buffer and began at the far corner of the room. The bristles made a soothing swishing sound, and the machine needed only the lightest touch to glide across the floor, leaving a shine in its wake. Melvin made his way past them.

"That's strange." Leah got up from the chair and went down on one knee.

"What is?" Melvin turned off his machine and knelt next to her.

"This was loose." Leah held up a thin strip of linoleum. "And it's clean cut all around."

"Why would someone do that?" Melvin took the piece from her and checked both sides of it.

"Beats me." Leah looked back down. "Wait." She picked up a small black disk dangling from a wire. "This is a microphone—my brother had one just like it, used it to bug my parents' room as a joke once." She shook her head. "They work pretty good."

"This place is bugged?" Melvin looked baffled.

"Should we call security?" Leah had the disk in her palm. "We'll at least need to report this."

"I'll take care of it." Melvin took the disk from her and dropped it into his pocket.

"Please let me know what they say," Leah said. "I've been here fifteen years and this is a new one on me."

"As soon as I know, you'll know." Melvin pointed to the floor. "I'll get some cement and fix that tile so no one gets hurt. Be right back." He left the room, the buffer rolling along behind him.

"Don't worry about this, Mr. Barnes." Leah patted his shoulder. "You just focus on getting better."

He wished a body could be fixed as easily as a broken tile.

CHAPTER 6

Julian dreamed he and Julia were up on a stage, dancing. The audience was men wearing sombreros, women in gaudy sarongs, and squealing children throwing popcorn footballs. The parents pointed at him and Julia. The children laughed. The curtain fell.

Julian rolled onto his side. Pain stabbed him, bringing him to consciousness.

An old man lay in the next bed, pale, mouth agape, cheeks hollow. A young woman who called him *Papa* was visiting him, her bony fingers counting rosary beads. Her words were indecipherable, but Julian found her tone soothing. She finished her prayer, rose from her chair, and kissed her father. Standing in the doorway, she smiled and waved at Julian before she left.

Julian heard muffled voices outside the door. The voices went silent, and then he heard a cough. He blinked.

A man with bushy salt-and-pepper hair and a thick body stood at the foot of his bed.

Julian reached for his whiteboard.

"No need for that, Barnes." The man's voice was gravelly, his mouth a grim line. He hooked something onto the bed railing, something curved and shiny—a silver cane.

Julian felt for the call button.

"Looking for this?" The man held the buzzer up. Cough. "Everything is fine, if you do as I say. If not, your girlfriend dies."

Julian wrote frantically.

WHAT? WHY?

"That's how I make sure you follow instructions." Cough.

Julian looked left. The door was closed. The old man in the next bed was still. The light above Julian went off.

"The staff is occupied." A hand came over Julian's mouth and knuckles dug into his broken ribs.

Excruciating pain—if he could have opened his mouth, he'd have screamed.

"It's amazing how little pressure is needed once you find the right spot."

Julian had tears in his eyes, but the wires held his mouth shut. This had to be a mistake.

"What?" The man finally removed his hand and stifled a cough. "Something you're trying to say?"

Julian grunted.

"Doesn't the pain make my point?" The man offered him the whiteboard. "You will *not* remember what happened the night of the accident. Understand?"

Julian didn't understand, not at all. But he nodded.

"Hire Milton Zorn, tell him you still don't remember, and settle with Wright as soon as you can. Story changes and your girlfriend dies." Cough. "Julia Rodgers. Found her on Facebook. She's a nice girl. But if you remember what happened, *she dies*. Got it?"

YES. He underlined it a bunch of times.

"Good. I'll be watching . . . and *listening*." Cough reached for his cane.

Listening—the bug! Cough probably put it in his room. Did he know they'd found it? Were there more?

Heart racing, he watched the man limp away.

Don't remember.

But why?

Maybe Wright was innocent and Cough had a vendetta against him. Then again, if Alan Wright was guilty, he had the most to lose if Julian remembered. Maybe Wright was guilty and hired Cough to make sure the truth didn't come out. The witness's account seemed to point toward Wright's guilt. And Julian was a careful driver—he couldn't believe he'd run that light.

But unless he *did* remember, he couldn't know for sure.

CHAPTER 7

Julian heard heels click on the floor. His eyes moved left.

Julia stood in the doorway wearing a pinstripe pantsuit. She'd come to see him every day he'd been in the hospital. His face felt flushed as he watched this beautiful businesswoman make her way over to him. He pushed a button and raised the back of his mattress to a forty-five degree angle.

"You feel better today, honey?" Her thumb ring tapped the railing on his bed as she leaned over him.

He rocked his trembling hand sideways.

"How'd you sleep last night?"

Don't remember or Julia dies.

He gave her a thumbs up. He couldn't tell her about Cough.

Her cool lips pressed his and lingered there. Then she moved the chair closer and sat.

She's beautiful.

He removed the cap on his marker. He wrote in the top corner of the whiteboard, having learned to use his writing space more judiciously.

YOU EAT?

"I came straight from work." She flipped open her cell. "Three more messages. Jeez." She folded her phone and shoved it back into her tiny pocketbook. "I'll grab a salad on the way home." Her eyes brightened. "A new place just opened, Sal's. They make an excellent eggplant Parmesan, just the way you like it." She looked toward the floor. "We'll go there as soon as you're better."

He imagined them eating together in an Italian restaurant, talking and laughing. The image darkened, dissolved. Would he ever get better?

"Don't worry, honey, you will." Not the first time she'd read his mind.

He looked left. The bed next to his was empty—his roommate had passed that morning. Dr. Halay had tried to revive him, shouting orders to Leah while he held paddles to the old man's chest. After five minutes, he gave up. It was the first time Julian saw someone die. Was the man's daughter relieved that he was now in a better place, or angry because he'd been taken from her?

DR. SAID I'D REMEMBER.

"Maybe it's better if you don't."

His stomach plummeted.

WHY WOULD YOU WANT THAT?

Her eyes drifted toward the foot of the bed.

"We can start fresh."

During their third month together, Julia had started to seem . . . ambivalent from time to time. One night when she seemed especially distant, he tried making love to her—passion had helped them before—but she said she was tired and suggested a rain check. He asked if there was someone else, or something he'd done to upset her. She said no to both and kissed him before rolling over and falling asleep. He watched her silhouette in the darkness for a long time that night, praying he wouldn't lose her.

Remember—

He gets into his car. The dashboard clock reads 7:30. Nothing after that.

YOU CALLED ZORN?

"Who's Zorn?"

ATTORNEY.

"What are you talking about?"

His stomach churned. Now he was positive: Evelyn had called Zorn, and Cough knew about Zorn because he'd bugged his room. It was the most plausible explanation.

"An attorney came to see you?" Julia said.

He nodded. HE'S RICH?

"Who?"

GUY WHO HIT ME.

"He's a brain surgeon," Julia said. "Wouldn't want him operating on me."

THERE'S A WITNESS. The lines faded, the marker low on ink.

"The attorney told you that?"

Julian nodded.

She looked confused. "And he said I sent him?"

HE MUST BE MISTAKEN. It had to be Evelyn—but he had to be certain before he told her.

Don't remember or Julia dies.

She wove their fingers together. He longed to feel her skin against his, her heart beating against his chest.

He opened the top drawer of the nightstand, pulled out Zorn's business card, and handed it to her. Then he erased the whiteboard and wrote.

PLEASE CALL HIM FOR ME.

CHAPTER 8

*"H*ey, big brother."

Julian looked up.

Tom was standing in the doorway in his usual attire: jeans, sneakers, and a black T-shirt. He sauntered over to the side of the bed.

Tears welled in Julian's eyes. It had been a while. He'd been meaning to call, but hadn't gotten around to it—too consumed by Julia. The realization hurt.

He picked up the whiteboard and snatched the marker off the mattress.

I WAS IN A CAR ACCIDENT.

"I heard." Tom scratched his scraggly beard. "A brain surgeon ran a red light. Damn, Julian, how do you feel? You look pretty banged up."

I'LL LIVE.

But would Julia? Her life was in his hands. He'd been

ordered not to remember, but he had to know the truth. Where to begin?

"The passenger in the other car died." Tom looked toward the floor. "It could've been you. You realize that?" Tom shook his head. "Man, I don't even want to think about what her family must be going through . . . what I'd be going through if it were me."

Julian had yet to see a picture of Cheryl Star, the woman Wright was involved with. She was a nurse, probably young and attractive. Her loved ones must be devastated. A sudden death, coming out of nowhere—those were always the toughest to take.

"Julia called me." Tom cracked a smile. "She sounds nice. I'm happy for you."

YOU TELL MOM ABOUT ME?

"No." Tom held up his palms. "Some things never change." He shrugged.

I'LL ASK JULIA TO CALL HER.

"Thanks." Tom had the grace to look embarrassed. "That's one thing I'd rather not deal with."

I UNDERSTAND.

"So what happened? Heck, the only time I ever remember you in trouble was when you lied to Mom about eavesdropping on one of our conversations." Tom slipped a toothpick into his mouth.

Julian remembered that—it had cost him a trip to the World Series. He swore he'd never lie again. For the most part, he'd been able to stick to it.

I CAN'T REMEMBER WHAT HAPPENED.

"The whole night?" Tom looked like he'd never seen his brother before.

THE PARTS THAT MATTER. He shivered.

"What's your last recollection?"

GOING TO JULIA'S.

The dashboard clock had read 7:30 p.m. just before he left his apartment. A whole hour of his life was missing.

"Julian, I know you like to handle things on your own, but if there's anything I can do . . ." Tom was smart, strong, a computer whiz, and the one person in the world Julian could trust to be there for him.

NEED YOUR—

He quickly erased the words.

Not yet, not until I know more.

"What?" Tom looked confused. "You need my help?"

ANOTHER TIME. TOO MUCH AT ONCE NOW.

"Okay, I get it." Tom stepped backward and grinned. "I know you. But if you need me, I'm here for you. Any time."

Julian knew this to be true as he watched Tom leave the room. When they were younger, he'd always protected Tom, who'd always looked up to him. Still did, though they weren't as close as they used to be.

At this point, he didn't even know what he'd ask Tom to do. If that changed, Tom would be the first person he'd look to. He was sure of that.

CHAPTER 9

Right after lunch the next day, a tall man in a gray suit walked into Julian's room. Another in a seemingly endless procession of visitors.

The man stood at the foot of the bed. He had a crew cut and dark piercing eyes. He didn't seem like the kind of guy you'd have a beer with unless you absolutely had to.

"Name's Slattery," he said. "Have some questions for you."

Julian's body felt hot. He wasn't ready for this.

"We need to file an accident report." Slattery sat, pulled out a pen and clicked it open. "Just a formality, nothing you need to be concerned with." He looked Julian up and down. "As long as you tell the truth."

Julian pointed to his mouth.

"'Yes' or 'no' answers are fine. If we need more, we have this." Slattery handed him the whiteboard. "And here's a brand-new marker." He held it up. "These are my favorite. Nice chiseled point."

Julian put the board on the table next to him and picked up the plastic cup. He sipped water through a straw. Some rolled down his chin.

"Your leg's broken?" Slattery slapped his own left leg. "I broke this one playing JV football. Still bothers me on rainy days." He took out a small spiral pad. "Do you remember what you were doing just before the accident?"

Julian shook his head. He didn't know what to make of this man, just sensed he was trouble.

"Think back. I'm sure the memory is there." Slattery appeared to search Julian's eyes. "Were you on your cell?"

Julian scowled. He hated distracted drivers. There were plenty of things he wasn't sure of, but whether he'd been on a cell wasn't one of them.

"Maybe you dropped something on the floor?" Slattery leaned closer. He had tobacco on his breath. "You only took your eyes off the road for a second. We all do that." He poked himself with his thumb. "Heck, I even do it once in a while."

Slattery seemed certain Julian was in the wrong. Could he be on Wright's payroll, too?

I'M A CAREFUL DRIVER.

"I see . . . So where were you going?"

The marker fell on the floor. Slattery picked it up and handed it to him. He grunted a thanks.

TO A FRIEND'S HOUSE.

"Who was this friend?" Slattery raised an eyebrow.

He couldn't trust this guy.

"Your friend . . . what's their name?" Slattery rubbed his jaw with nicotine-stained fingers.

Julian stared at the wall in front of him.

"The truth comes out eventually," Slattery said. "Do us a favor and start with it."

JULIA. His hand trembled as he wrote this. Slattery seemed to notice.

"Julia? Is she your girlfriend?"

He nodded.

"Does your girlfriend have a last name?"

RODGERS. He felt as if he'd just implicated Julia in a crime.

"What happened when you got there?"

DON'T KNOW IF I DID.

An image flashed in Julian's mind. Women's backs. They vanished.

"What's your girlfriend's address?"

He scrawled 2575 PALISADES AVE on the board.

"The accident was at the corner of Wendt and Brewster. You were heading west—you must have been leaving her apartment. Your girlfriend hasn't mentioned you being there?"

His heart beat faster. He closed his eyes and turned his head to the side.

"You're tired. How about I give you a few minutes to rest?"

He opened his eyes. Best to get this over with.

"So, Julia did mention it?" Slattery stared at him.

DID NOT. Julian underlined the second word.

"Did not." Slattery made a notation. "Was it possible you two had a fight? I've been married twenty-five years and sometimes Alice and I really get into it. When I was your age I did some crazy stuff when I got angry."

NO FIGHT.

"You sound awfully sure for someone who can't remember."

WE DON'T FIGHT.

"You know anything about the man who allegedly ran into you?"

HE'S A BAD DRIVER.

"You'd better get your facts straight if you plan to sue." Slattery's jaw tightened. "Dr. Wright has saved a lot of lives. He'll go on saving more as long as he's not incarcerated for a crime he says he didn't commit."

"Oh, I'm sorry." They both looked up—Julia stood in the doorway. "I didn't know you had company."

"You must be Ms. Rodgers?"

"Yes."

"Name's Slattery." He held up his pad. "Just filling out an accident report."

"Are you with the police?"

"I'm an investigator. Julian and I were just wondering what were you doing at the time of the accident?"

Julian groaned, wishing he could tell her not to say a word until they communicated first.

"I was home," Julia said.

"Were you alone?"

"No."

Julian did a double take. She was with someone?

"Who were you with?" Slattery said.

"A friend." Her gaze dropped to the floor. "That's all."

There weren't a lot of people Julian trusted, and Julia was one of them. But now she seemed nervous, and that would make Slattery suspicious, which meant more questions.

"When were you with your *friend*?" Slattery said.

"We were there until about nine." She tented her fingers.

"So you didn't see Julian at your apartment?"

"No. I saw him at the hospital, in the emergency room."

Julian tried to remain calm.

Remember—

He is on a stretcher. Red lights flash and people yell. The left side of his body is in searing pain. He's struggling to breathe. Julia comes toward him. He thinks it's a hallucination until she takes his hand and stays with him as they wheel him down a corridor.

Just then, Dr. Halay entered the room.

"Quite a crowd we have here." He picked up Julian's chart and turned a page.

"Any idea when Mr. Barnes might get his memory back?" Slattery looked over the doctor's shoulder.

"I don't believe it's a long-term situation." Halay glanced at the investigator. "Though you can never be sure with these things."

"Well, Doctor, I'd better let you attend to your patient." Slattery stared at Julian. "I'll be back." His gaze rested on Julia for a moment. "And nice meeting you, Ms. Rodgers."

CHAPTER 10

Julian was surrounded by white. The sheet that covered him, the gown that clothed him, the walls that surrounded him. Even the board he used to communicate with the rest of the world was white.

He had to get out of here. This place was making his skin crawl. Death lurking all around him, claiming souls at random. He'd never been a patient in a hospital, never had so many people giving him attention. He wanted to wear regular clothes again. It would be nice to not have an exposed backside—a pair of jeans would do him good. Too bad he'd have to cut open the leg on his oldest pair to accommodate the cast.

Remember—

He's at Julia's, 8 p.m. A half-hour—that's how long it takes to get there. He leans forward with both hands on the wheel as he drives past her building. Her car is parked in front. He chuckles. She got a good space—they're at a premium in this neighborhood.

At the corner, he turns left and finally finds a spot halfway down on the right. He parks, locks his car, and heads toward her apartment. When he gets there he puts his hand on the hood of her car. It's warm. He's surprised—on Fridays she usually ends the week early with a glass of Chianti and a hot bath. The hairs on his arms rise. Something isn't right.

Julian opened his eyes. Blinding sunlight poured into the room.

"Hello, Julian," Julia's mother said.

He pulled up the blanket. How long had she been there?

"You were asleep. I didn't want to disturb you." Ruth Rodgers had long dark hair just like her daughter's and the same captivating blue eyes. She'd become a widow not long after her youngest was born and raised her two daughters on her own while working as an attorney. Most of her clients were battered wives. "Julia's at work. I told her I'd stop by. Hope you don't mind a little company?"

GOOD TO SEE YOU.

"Hello." Dina, Julia's older sister, walked into the room. Her husband, Reed, was behind her. Dina had Julia's height and build, but her hair was blond and her eyes green. She was an avid runner, didn't eat red meat, and volunteered at a local soup kitchen. Reed was the CEO of an up-and-coming technology firm. He patted Julian's shoulder. Dina kissed his cheek.

"I broke my jaw playing soccer in college," Reed said. "It's not pleasant. I'll send you this great whey protein I discovered. You'll need it for a while."

"And once you can chew again," Dina said, "I promise we'll have you over for dinner."

He had a keen appreciation of Dina's exceptional culinary skills.

THANK YOU BOTH.

"We'll get together in better times." Reed checked his watch. His cell phone began playing Mozart's *A Little Night Music*. He silenced it.

"We're going to head out." Dina kissed his other cheek. "It was good to see you, Julian. Hope you feel better soon."

"Take care of that jaw." Reed shook his hand. "I'll get you that whey protein."

"Mom, we'll see you in the parking lot." Dina left. Reed waved and followed her out.

Ruth pulled up a chair.

"I wanted a minute alone with you," she said.

His pulse picked up.

"My daughter and I don't agree on everything—I'm liberal and she's turning into a Republican—but we agree about you."

He was taken aback. He never had the feeling Ruth had particularly approved of him, but that was understandable— she just wanted the best for her youngest daughter.

"Julia loves you," Ruth said.

I LOVE HER.

"I know." Ruth gently took his hand. "You make her happy and content. She wasn't that way with her last boyfriend."

Julian shifted, uncomfortable. All he knew about Richard was that he was handsome, an architect, a genius—and moody. He and Julia never really talked about their previous relationships, but he knew Richard had hurt her.

"I'll let you rest." Ruth got up and walked to the door but stopped and turned back. Her eyes were rheumy.

"When Julia was a little girl, she could play with a ball for hours, in a corner, all by herself. But if it ever rolled away from her, she wouldn't bother to get it. One day I asked her why she didn't go pick it up. She giggled and said, 'I'm practicing letting things go.'" Ruth shook her head. "Out of the mouths of babes."

Julian nodded and wondered where this was leading.

"At the time, I thought that was a good thing. There's so much we hang on to that we'd be better off releasing. Still, there are things we should hold on to." Ruth looked directly into his eyes. "It would be a sin if the two of you didn't wind up together." She wiped the corner of her eye. "I've said enough. Feel better soon."

He stared at the now-vacant doorway.

What was Ruth trying to tell him that she hadn't said?

———

Julian had been asleep when the light above his head came on, blindingly bright.

A figure limped away from him. Salt–and–pepper hair and a broad back were all he saw as Cough disappeared into the dimness at the foot of the bed.

Julian tensed.

"Relax, Mr. Barnes, I'm not going to hurt you." Cough. "I've made my point."

Julian barely saw his face.

"I'm a little sad today."

WHY?

"Memories." Cough, cough. "They're bad because they're good."

WHAT DO YOU WANT FROM ME?

"Stick to your story. Can you do that?"

I REALLY DON'T REMEMBER.

"That's not the point!" Cough. "I need to know you understand I'm serious."

UNDERSTAND. The letters were shaky.

"Good." Cough stood up. "Now go live your life, Mr. Barnes. And make sure Julia keeps on living hers."

CHAPTER 11

"**H**ey," Julian said. "Still up for some company?"

He was driving, talking to Julia on the cell phone hands-free.

"That would be great." She sounded happy, the way he always wished she would be—the way he was when he was with *her*.

They still hadn't talked about what had happened that night. At first he'd wanted to wait until he could speak. Then he decided to wait until the cast came off and he could literally stand on his own two feet. Now that both those things had happened, he had to face the fact that he was procrastinating because he didn't want to risk ruining what they now had.

The deposition still loomed over them. Until then, he'd savor their time together.

"How's your headache?" Julian said.

"Gone when I woke this morning. Can't remember the last time I had one that bad."

"You've been getting them a lot lately."

"I know." She sighed.

"Maybe you should see a doctor?" His unsteady words took him by surprise.

"I will," she said. "When I'm ready."

"I have a friend, college roommate—he's a neurologist," Julian said. "Couldn't hurt."

"Can I think about it?"

"Julia, I don't want to pressure you, but you really should get it checked out."

"I promise I'll see someone when I feel it's necessary. Do you trust me to do that?"

"Of course." But he sensed this wasn't the last time they'd discuss this.

"Let's talk about something fun. How's the new car?"

"It looks a lot like the old one." He'd bought the same model he'd leased previously, hoping that driving it might elicit memories of the accident. It was the first large-ticket purchase he'd made since finding out he'd soon be a millionaire.

"You should be more excited, honey. You deserve it."

So why didn't he feel like he deserved it?

"I'll see you at nine," he said. "That excites me."

"I can't wait."

He imagined kissing her, touching her, holding her close. Things had changed between them—for the better. Back during Julia's "existential ambivalence," as she described it, she'd told him she hated her mishmash of feelings. Now they were in love, he as much as she, the way he'd always known they could be.

He arrived at Julia's and parked. He opened the car door, got out, and felt a stab of pain in his left thigh. This always came when he stood—a remnant from the accident.

He looked at the apartment building in front of him. It was eighteen stories high, across from the Palisades. Most of the windows were lit. He headed toward the front of the building, entered the vestibule, and hit the button on the elevator. The doors slid aside.

He relaxed a little. The elevator hadn't been waiting the night of the accident.

He pressed "3" and the cab started moving. Muzak played softly. He tapped his foot. His shirt was rough on his neck. He ran his finger under the collar. The car stopped, the doors parted.

Julia stood there, wearing a red raincoat and high heels. She entered the cab. Her eyes sparkled, her lips glistened, and her hair smelled fresh. She pressed the button for the first floor.

"I've got a craving for souvlaki." She pecked his lips. "Let's go to that little Greek place by you."

"Why go all the way over there when Zorba's is right here?"

"It's not that far." She nestled next to him. "We'll be there in no time. Besides, we can head back to your place after."

He held her tighter.

"I'll get my car and follow you." She looked up at him. "I can go to work from there in the morning."

"Perfect." His stomach growled. "Let's go. I'm hungry."

They held hands as they walked out the door.

———

"You're shivering," Julian said as they lay in bed the next morning.

"I'm always cold lately." Julia rubbed her neck. When he took over, she bowed her head. "Harder."

"I don't want to hurt you."

"I'll let you know if you do." She touched his hand. "I've got a terrible headache."

He massaged deeper.

"That feels *so* good, you have no idea. Please don't stop. Your fingers work magic. Has anyone else ever told you that?"

"No."

"Well, they do—they always have."

Her muscles slowly yielded under his thumbs. He loved this woman. He'd never love another one like this, didn't want to ever have to try.

"Thank you," she said after a while. "You healed me."

"I still think you need to see a doctor."

"Julian, don't scare me."

"I'm not trying to. I just love you and don't want anything to happen to you." Was he wrong about this? He didn't think so.

"I know. It's just that I need to do it my way. Like you do with your amnesia."

Remember—

He enters the building. No elevator is waiting. He takes the steps two at a time—

"Are you thinking about that night?" she said.

"Yes . . . I still can't remember the parts that matter."

"Maybe it's better if you don't."

Don't remember or Julia dies.

He curled into a fetal position as he cowered on his side of the bed.

"Hon, are you okay?" She came over to him.

"Yes." He held her gently. "Why . . . why would you think it's better if I never recall what happened that night?"

"I want things to stay the way they are right now."

"And they will, I promise. But I have to find out the truth."

Julia dies.

He covered his ears.

"Hon, is something wrong?" She stared at him.

"No." He held up his hands. "It's okay . . . I guess I could use a vacation."

"Let's go to Jamaica."

"What?"

"We both need a rest." She knelt on the bed and sat back on her heels. "Just you and me."

"I've got the deposition."

"We don't have to stay long. It'll do us both good." She stroked his chest. "What do you say?"

He imagined them lying on a beach under a searing sun, listening to the soothing sound of the surf and enjoying a balmy breeze.

"Sure." He'd make her happy and could use the rest. "Let's go for a few days. We'll fly back in time for the deposition."

"Perfect." She got off the bed and picked up her tablet. Her fingers played on its surface. "I'll see what's available."

He checked his watch.

"I've got to see Zorn and sign the last of the papers. It won't take long."

"I'll be here."

———

Zorn was at his desk reading. Pictures of the attorney with various celebrities covered half the wall behind him. His credentials filled the other half.

"Julian." Zorn rose. They shook hands. "Nice to see you up and about. How are you feeling?"

"I've healed, for the most part."

"Good to hear." Zorn handed him a check for one million dollars. "Wright paid my fee, so it's the full amount. All you need to do is sign this release form."

Julian put his pen on the page. It didn't move.

"Everything okay?" Zorn said.

"Yes." He affixed his signature and dated it. He slipped the check into an envelope and dropped it in his inside pocket. He shook Zorn's hand.

"You're a good person, Julian," Zorn said. "I wish you and Julia a life of happily ever after and hope this settlement money facilitates that."

"I plan on investing it and living off the interest."

"Sounds like a good plan." Zorn patted him on the back.

Julian turned to go. He'd deposit the money in the bank as soon as he left.

"Julian?" Zorn said. "I've meant to ask you, did you ever find out who left me that message initially?"

"Someone I know." He wanted to tell him he thought it was Evelyn, but maybe it was better to put this issue behind him. "It was a misunderstanding on my part."

Zorn held his gaze for a minute. Julian wasn't an adroit liar, but lately he'd had no choice.

"Call me if you need me," Zorn said.

"Hopefully I won't." He liked his attorney but hoped never to need him again.

CHAPTER 12

The airport was empty at 6 a.m. Julia was walking next to him, still half-asleep. She wasn't a morning person but had agreed it would be better to leave early to avoid any chance of delay. They both wanted to make the most of the few days they'd have together.

They went right up to the counter with their bags. He handed their tickets to the attendant, a woman in her twenties with short dark hair.

"Sorry, sir." She had a finger on the screen in front of her, pointing to a line he could see but not read. "That flight is delayed due to a mechanical problem."

"How long?" He couldn't believe it.

The woman was typing. "We're still waiting for a report from maintenance. I'll send them a follow-up request. Better here than up there." She pointed to the ceiling. "Besides, it may not be too long. In the meantime, I can check your bags."

"Thank you." He lifted their luggage and placed it on the tray adjacent to the counter. Julia's duffel bag was a duplicate of his.

"Matching bags and almost-matching first names." The attendant smiled as she processed them. "Gate 7." She handed him their boarding passes and they headed toward security.

Julia rubbed her temples and came to a halt. He stopped short so he didn't run into her.

"You okay?" He peered at her.

"Another headache."

"When did—"

"Not now. We'll deal with it after we get back . . . if it's still a problem. Now is about having a good time."

"I'm taking you to a doctor as soon as we get back."

"Fair enough." She sounded tired. "Now let's go. I'm looking forward to lying on the beach with you."

———

Julian was stretched out in a lounge chair. Julia was lying next to him in a black bikini, sunglasses propped on top of her head as she read one of her journals. She'd cut her hair short, said it was a new beginning. He had to admit he liked the look.

"This is perfect," she said.

"It is." He studied her long slender body and recalled making love to her the night before. They'd been in the hot tub. It was late. No one was around when Julia slid off her bikini bottoms and helped him out of his trunks.

Now it was just after eleven. The sun was hot, the air

humid. Thunderstorms were supposed to roll in around one, but as the locals would say, "Hey, mon, if you don't like the weather here, wait a few minutes."

"Thanks for suggesting this," he said. "I needed it."

She smiled. "I know."

A tall man wearing a wide straw hat and a colorful shirt bounded toward them. His tremendous fingers balanced two banana daiquiris on a tray. They both sat up as he approached.

"These cool you off." The waiter handed one daiquiri to Julia and the other to Julian and then extended one of his sinewy arms toward the shore. "Plenty to do on the island. My name is Paso. If there is *anything* you need, please ask me."

"Thanks," Julian said.

There was a stretch of silence. Sea gulls strutted along the beach. Paso nodded, turned, and left.

"How's your course in journaling going?" Julian said once they were alone.

Julia sat on the edge of her lounge chair. "It's been therapeutic." She dug her toes into the alabaster grains.

"How so?" His hand was on her thigh. She caressed his.

"It helps me see problems from other perspectives. Ways I wouldn't have if I hadn't put it down in black and white."

"And that helps you make better decisions?" For the thousandth time, he wondered how he was lucky enough to be with this woman. Her brain was as beautiful as she was.

"Pretty much," she said. "I guess I need structure in order to facilitate that. One of my flaws."

"Not necessarily."

They kissed.

It was the first time they'd been away together, just the two of them, no distractions. He imagined their honeymoon, their first night as man and wife. Whoa—he was getting ahead of himself. Still, it was a nice thought. He hoped it happened one day. One day soon.

Clouds rolled toward them from the horizon. The sun cut in and out. The ocean went from green to blue. There was a bamboo bar near the entrance to the beach. It had a thatched roof and was open on all sides. A middle-aged man sat on the edge of a stool and nursed a beer. The man looked familiar, but Julian couldn't place him. Maybe when they were checking in? Or maybe on the plane? Since the accident, strangers often looked familiar and the people he knew looked like strangers.

Julia locked her fingers with his, sighed, and closed her eyes as if she sensed what he sensed—this was a moment to hold on to.

"How's your headache?" he said.

"Better, and there'll be no more for the rest of this vacation." She stretched her arms above her head. "Mind putting some suntan lotion on me?"

"Not at all." He jumped up.

She unhooked the strap on her bathing suit and draped her arms over the back of the lounge chair. Her fingers grazed the white sand.

He grabbed a brown bottle, poured the slick liquid onto her back, and rubbed it in. Her muscles were firm, her skin soft and smooth. He loved her back.

A scene flashed in his mind, not for the first time—women sitting on pedestals, lined up in a row with their backs to him. They turned around in unison. Each of them was beautiful. Each was Julia.

"That feels wonderful," she said as he worked the oil into her shoulders. She'd been all-city in swimming in high school and still had the body to prove it.

He squirted a line of oil onto each of her calves.

She raised her head. "Thank you." Her skin was still tan from last summer. Still working on his, he had to take it slower than Julia. He burned easily.

He moved on to her thighs and looked around. A woman was reading a paperback, the bald man with her a newspaper. Two young men played Frisbee, watched by two young women sitting cross-legged on a blanket sharing a hand-rolled cigarette.

Julian slid his hand between Julia's legs.

She breathed deep. He went higher. She moaned and then pushed herself up with one hand and with the other hand held her top against her breasts.

"Would you like to go back to the room?" she said.

"I just put oil on you." His fingers were still greasy.

"Then you've got to stop . . . for now."

"Sorry."

"Don't be." She let her top fall and held him close. "We've got time, right?"

"Absolutely." He kissed her neck. Warm sun caressed his face. His broken leg and ribs had healed, he was set financially for life, and he was with the woman he loved. Everything was right.

So long as he didn't remember—

"Let's go back to Andreas tonight for dinner." She held his hand. "I can still taste the filet mignon, and that chocolate lava cake was amazing." She smiled. "And us together in the whirlpool afterward . . . I want the same experience all over again."

"If that's what you want, that's what we'll do."

Maybe things would work out after all? Even if he remembered, he didn't have to tell anybody.

That's when he looked up and saw Slattery standing by the bamboo bar, beckoning him.

———

"Nice to see you looking so well." Slattery was wearing wing-tipped shoes, long dark pants, and a white short-sleeve shirt. He flattened his collar. "Guess I need to dress more appropriately."

"You're here on *vacation?*"

"Strictly business."

Julian had told Julia he was going for a walk and would be back in ten minutes. He'd tell her about Slattery later, after they got home. If he told her before, it would spoil the rest of their vacation. She'd understand.

He checked over his shoulder. Julia was still on her lounger, facedown with her headphones on. He turned back to Slattery.

"What do you want?" His hands were fists.

"Let's go for a stroll." Slattery led him to a wooden

walkway. They went left at the end of it and headed down a narrow asphalt path. It was hot. "Some men gamble." Slattery shielded his eyes. "Others watch sports. Me, I'm into the truth. Sometimes I wish I wasn't. Sometimes I wish I was just a regular guy." His gaze lingered on two attractive women in heels and string bikinis as they made their way around them. "But in the end, we are who we are."

"I've got to go." Julian's soles had been burned by the pavement. He stepped off the path and onto grass that ran along it.

Slattery moved in front of him.

"Who do you work for?" Julian said.

"Alan Wright. He's a friend, saved my mother's life. He could be tried for manslaughter." Slattery shook his head slowly. "If he's innocent, that's a crime."

"So you're not a cop?"

"Was."

"The witness said it was Wright's fault."

"He's mistaken. We're going to prove it."

Julian felt dizzy. He leaned on a picnic table.

Don't remember or Julia dies.

The image of women's backs resurfaced in his head. The women turned in unison and smiled—they had no teeth. They laughed and melted on their pedestals.

"You know Richard Fontaine?" Slattery's stogie fell to the ground.

He twitched. "Yes."

"He's dead." Slattery stomped on the cigar, picked up the squashed butt, and tossed it into a trash can.

"He's Julia's ex-boyfriend. What does that have to do with anything?" He tried to appear calm.

"Fontaine died the night of your accident."

"How?"

"Heart attack . . . It happened in Julia's apartment."

Julian felt like he'd just taken a punch to the gut.

"One good piece of news," Slattery said. "There was *no* foul play."

Julia had said she was with a friend. Why hadn't she told him it was Richard—that her ex-lover had a heart attack in her apartment?

"That's probably enough to hit you with for now. We'll talk more later." Slattery turned and walked away.

CHAPTER 13

Julian woke. Julia was asleep next to him, a sheet wrapped around her, one thigh exposed. He kissed her hair, took in her fresh scent. She turned away. His fingers massaged the nape of her neck and then followed the curve of her spine toward her buttocks.

He stopped. Richard was dead. Why hadn't Julia told him? It had to be eating her up even though she didn't show it.

Maybe it's better if you don't remember.

His hand hovered above her, ready to wake her. Had she cheated on him? He tried to picture himself with another woman— couldn't. He and Julia were a lot alike.

He pulled his hand back and let her sleep. Better do a little research first. Right now all he had was Slattery's word.

Faint island music crept into the room—steel drums, horns, a xylophone—carefree sounds. There was laughter in the hallway, then shouts.

"Be quiet." A woman's voice, then giggling. Footsteps came closer—one set definitely heavier. "Shush. Not here." A moment later, a door closed. Then another slammed shut. Firecrackers sounded like a machine gun in the night.

"Hey." Julia was awake. She grabbed his wrist and pulled him closer.

They kissed—long and deep, their bodies pressed against one another. His lips moved down her soft, supple skin.

The image of the women's backs appeared in his mind. They turned around in unison—faces all Julia's.

Richard could have shown up unexpectedly. Something he'd left at her apartment, maybe? She offers him something to drink and returns to find him expired on her couch. Simple as that—he had no reason to believe otherwise.

Except that she'd kept it from him.

Now her lips caressed his chest. His senses screamed. Straddling him, she slipped him inside her. He ran his fingers lightly over her breasts and kissed them, lips lingering on each nipple. She closed her eyes and rubbed her body over his, moaning. Her movement intensified. She bit her lip. He pushed up, going deeper. Her moan morphed into a wail, then a scream. He let go.

Julia collapsed on top of him and rested her head on his chest. He listened to her breathing, felt her rapid heartbeat. He put his arm around her.

He knew he loved her. He just didn't know if he could trust her.

—

A fan lazily rotated above Julian, mixing the cool air. The lobby was crowded, people everywhere. A young man in a well-cut suit strode past him. Julian knew what he had to do. Julia was upstairs getting dressed. That would give him the opportunity he needed.

Slattery appeared, as if out of nowhere. Julian rocked back on his heels.

"You like?" Slattery spun around, showing off sandals, black cargo shorts, and a pink collared shirt littered with palm trees and flamingos.

"Better." Julian pictured having a drink with this man, getting to the bottom of things, persuading Slattery to tell him what was really going on. The vision darkened, dissolved. "When we met, you said you were a detective," Julian said. "You lied to me."

"I feel bad about that." He looked genuinely regretful. "From now on I'll be straight with you as long as you're straight with me."

Julian still wasn't sure he could trust Slattery, but he couldn't get much further on his own.

"Catch you later." Slattery's hand formed a pistol he fired at Julian. Then he headed out the door.

Julian waited five minutes. When Slattery didn't reappear, he made a left and read a sign that said the computer center was straight ahead.

He went down the long narrow hallway. A door was open on his right. Inside, a maid tucked a sheet under a mattress. She met his gaze. A boy ran toward him, arms spread, screaming. A woman followed, yelling "Jonathan!"

Julian picked up his pace. When he got to the end of the hall, he came to a glass door. He looked in. A computer was inside, cursor blinking on the blank monitor.

He sucked in a breath. He could stop right here. Forget the past. He and Julia could start over, like she wanted to.

He reached into his wallet, removed his key card, and slid it into the door slot. The green light lit. Click. He turned the door's handle, pulled, and went inside.

He sat at the computer. A laser printer was next to it, printing blank pages. He opened the browser and typed *Richard Fontaine.* A link appeared. He clicked on it.

An article, two years old. A picture of Richard in front of a sleek, pointed black building. He was leaning against a pole. The soft glow of a streetlight rained down on him. He had a confident expression on his handsome face. The caption read: "Richard Fontaine—Focused on Form and Functionality."

Julian clicked the browser's "back" button. There was another story in a local paper: "Architect Dies Unexpectedly." It said Richard Fontaine was DOA at Sunrise Hospital on Friday, October 2, 2009. They mentioned his notable accomplishments and quoted a fellow architect: "He was the twenty-first century's Howard Roark."

Sweat from his forehead seeped into Julian's eyes. Slattery said there'd been no foul play. The article didn't mention the cause of death. He had no reason to believe Richard's demise wasn't natural.

So why didn't she tell you?

He had to know.

———

Julian jogged down the hall to their room, panting as he tried to put together the words he'd use. Suddenly he remembered what Ruth had said: "You make her happy and content. Not the way she was with her last boyfriend." She knew something.

Julian pulled out his cell and started dialing, paused on the last digit, entered it.

"Julian," Ruth said after the second ring. "I thought you two were in Jamaica?"

"We are."

"Is everything all right?"

"Yes. It's just . . ." What to say? "Julia seems to have something on her mind."

"She usually does," Ruth said. "Can't say I know half of what she's thinking. And I've learned over the years it's better to wait for her to share rather than attempt to pry it out of her. You force her and she'll close up tighter than a clam."

"Thanks. I'll keep that in mind." He switched the phone to his other hand. There was silence on the line.

"Was there something you wanted to ask me?" Ruth said.

"I did want to know if . . . You know what, never mind. You've given me enough already. It's up to us to work out the rest."

"You make Julia happy. She's a complicated girl and a wonderful human being."

"I love her, Mrs. Rodgers."

"I know you do, and she loves you."

"Thanks. Good night, Mrs. Rodgers."

"Good night, Julian."

The conversation played in his head as he walked the rest of the hallway. He came to their room and went in. It was dark.

Julia was on the floor in a fetal position. Julian rushed to her and knelt beside her.

"My head is killing me," she said. "I'm scared."

"I'm here."

"I love you *so* much." She tightened her grip on him.

There was a knock.

"Who is it?" He glanced toward the door.

"It's Slattery." A voice from the hall.

"He can't come in here." Julia didn't seem surprised by the fact that the investigator was in Jamaica. "Not now."

He spoke to the door. "Julia's not dressed."

"I can wait." Slattery sounded louder. "This is important."

Julia shook her head.

"Sorry, Slattery," Julian said. "She's not feeling well. We'll have to do this another time. Soon, but another time."

"Stop harassing us." Julia held Julian's hand. "I saw you interrogating him on the beach."

"Ms. Rodgers, if it's not me, it'll be someone else."

"What are you talking about?" Julia said.

"You need to see what I have, Ms. Rodgers. Both of you do."
Julia retied her robe. "Let him in," she said.

Julian opened the door. Slattery handed him a black binder. The cover read "Wendt and Brewster Stoplight Analysis."

"It's a little extensive," Slattery said. "But you being a numbers guy, I think you'll appreciate it. See, we recently found out Wright's car had a black box, like on an airplane. So now we know the exact moment of the crash. That enabled us to figure out what color the light was based on how it was programmed. Go on. Have a look."

There were a series of tabs. One had a detailed explanation of the calculation used to determine what color a stoplight would be at any given second. Behind another tab was a projection of what color the light at Wendt and Brewster had been at any given second on October 2, 2009. There was a summary chart and a list of assumptions. It had been prepared by an outside consulting firm Julian had heard of.

"This *is* extensive." Julian kept turning pages.

"What does it say?" Julia said.

"There's a 96 percent chance I ran that light." He held up the binder, his finger on the top page. "Ninety-six point two, to be exact."

"I'm going to lose you?" She looked up at him.

"Why'd you involve Julia in this?" Julian said.

"I'm not the bad guy here." Slattery pointed to the binder. "A good man is being falsely accused. You need to remember what happened so we can get this straightened out as soon as possible. Lives are at stake."

"Whose lives?" Julia's fingers pressed her temples.

"Patients who could be saved." Slattery stared at Julian. "You still don't remember?"

Slattery wanted him to remember. Cough wanted him to forget. They couldn't be co-conspirators. Slattery said he worked for Wright—which meant Cough didn't.

So who was Cough, and why didn't he want Julian to remember?

"I'll leave you two alone for now." Slattery walked toward the door, grabbed the handle, and stopped. "And just some advice . . . I wouldn't spend the money. If you're guilty, you'll want to give it back."

Julian figured that was the least of his problems.

———

As soon as Slattery left, Julia plopped down on the bed. "Something is wrong," she said. "Really wrong. It's getting worse. Everything makes me nauseous, even me."

He sat next to her, his arm around her.

"And this blind spot." She dabbed her eyes with the tissue. "Julian, this is bad."

"I'll call Nellie and get you in ASAP." He held her closer.

She leaned into him. "I've never felt so vulnerable." Tears streaked her cheeks.

"I'm here."

"For now." She let go. "I was such a fool for the time I wasted with you."

"Don't say that."

"Julian, that night . . ." She sniffled and clutched the tissue. She was pale, her nose raw. She was still beautiful.

"Let's . . . forget about that, for now." His fingers combed her hair, untangling it. "There are more pressing things for us to deal with."

"All right." She staggered to her feet. "We should pack. The shuttle comes at noon."

CHAPTER 14

Julian drove Dina's luxury SUV along a snaking country road. The vehicle was so high above the ground that he felt like they were riding on air.

"Turn left at the next corner." Julia was in the passenger seat.

His body felt heavy and the back of his eyelids were sandpaper. He was in desperate need of a shower and a good night's sleep after the flight and the dinner they'd just had with Dina, Reed, and their two kids. But he knew Julia wouldn't rest until she saw her mother.

A car approached from around a bend. He switched off his high beams and then sipped from the travel mug Dina had given him. Excellent coffee—not too bitter, smooth all the way down.

They passed a sign for the town of Winthrop, founded in 1868. It had cobblestone streets lined with quaint restaurants and shops. People strolled the sidewalk under the glow of street lamps. He imagined walking along these sidewalks with Julia, holding hands as they each pushed a baby carriage—a boy in his and a girl in hers.

"Whatever's wrong with me is serious, Julian."

He put his hand on hers.

"You saw it sooner than I did." She bowed her head. "I'm sorry I was so stubborn."

"You were in denial. I understand." He glanced in the rearview mirror, both hands back clutching the wheel. "Are you going to tell your mother?"

"I'm worried about what it's going do to her."

"Why?"

"She's going to have to be there for me." Julia crossed her arms. "It'll take a lot out of her, and I feel bad about that."

Julia was sick. He was still getting used to that. His heart beat faster as he entered a wide driveway.

He put the vehicle in "park" and looked up at the huge stone Tudor in front of them as Julia fished a set of keys from her pocketbook.

"Let's go." She pulled the door handle.

They got out of the car and held hands as they walked a slate path lined with lamps.

"These lights weren't here when I was a kid." She tapped her jaw. "I have a scar from falling because they weren't. My mother installed them the day after it happened."

"I'm scarred under my jaw from falling on a radiator." He showed her the mark.

She reached up and touched it. "How did I miss that?"

They came to an arched wood door with a big brass knocker. Julia slid a key into the lock, turned it, and pushed the door. They stepped inside.

The foyer was dark, the air nippy. She flipped a switch. A crystal chandelier came on. It hung above them from a high ceiling. She looked up at it and spun around.

"I used to do this when I was a kid." She stopped. "Whew, I'm dizzy."

"That can't be good for your headaches." He stuck out his arm and she used it to steady herself.

"I don't care . . . just for tonight."

He understood.

Candle-shaped lights lined the hallway ahead of them. At the bottom of the stairs was a suit of armor.

"Those are expensive." He'd thought about owning one someday.

"You can touch it."

The metal felt cool and sturdy, the lance was solid.

"My mother said Dad had a fit the day she bought it. But he loved her and always gave in to her . . . eventually, according to her." She switched on the light for the second floor. "Let's go to my room." She led him past crossed swords mounted on the wall. "Those always creeped me out."

He was about to agree when he heard a squeak. "What was that?" he said.

"Don't know."

They continued up the stairs and came to five doors, all closed.

"This is my mom's room." They walked past it. "This was Dina's." They passed a green door and went toward a white one. She opened it and hesitated before she stepped inside. He followed her in.

The room was painted sky blue. A movie poster for *Casablanca* was taped on one wall, a picture of a rolling brook with a bench beside it on another.

Julia slid open the mirrored doors on the closet. Clothes still hung there, and shoes lined the floor. She pulled out a dress. "I wore this to my high school prom." He watched her reflection in the mirror as she held the short electric blue garment against her. He wished he'd taken her to her prom.

"I wish I knew you then and went with you," she said as she returned the dress to the closet.

"I was just thinking the same thing."

"We do that a lot." She got on her knees and rummaged through shoes.

"It's why we're so good together."

"You're right." She gazed up at him, and he dropped to his knees beside her.

"Are you searching for something in particular?"

"Memories." She sat back on her heels. "I want as many as I can get. You know, recalling your past helps you cope with an uncertain future?"

"I do."

"I wore these to my sweet sixteen." She held up a pair of shoes. "We'd be less scarred if we'd found each other sooner."

"Try the dress on," he said.

"Huh?"

"Your prom dress—try it on. I want to see you in it."

They both stood. She unbuttoned her shirt and it fell to the floor. As she slipped out of her jeans, he resisted an urge to take her in his arms and make love to her. She removed her bra.

"Can't wear one with that dress." She stepped out of her panties. "Need a thong or it's nothing."

Naked, she retrieved the dress from the closet, pulled down the zipper, and stepped into it. The material slid over her body, conforming to it as it covered her. She slipped on one slender shoulder strap, then the other. Barefoot, she padded over to him and showed him her back. He zipped her up. She went up on her toes and modeled it for him.

"How do I look?" She spun around.

"Perfect."

She blushed.

He sees himself in an electric blue suit, standing in front of a door. He rings the bell. Julia appears wearing her dress—matching colors. They laugh, then he presents her with a corsage and plants a kiss on her cheek.

He was lonely as a teenager. Those years would have been so much better if he'd been with her.

Her cell phone rang. She picked up. Moments later, her hand was over the mouthpiece.

"It's Dina—Mom forgot her keys. Dina told her we were here."

The doorbell rang. They looked at each other.

"I'll answer it," he said on his way out of the room. "Give you time to get dressed."

———

Julian opened the door. Ruth was standing there in a black dress and heels, carrying an attaché case. She kissed his check and stepped past him.

Julia ran down the stairs, back in her jeans and shirt.

"Mom." Julia kissed her.

"Baby." Ruth put her arm around her daughter and they entered the living room together. Ruth sat on the couch. "My feet are killing me." She kicked off her heels, stretched out her slender legs, and wiggled her toes. "Been wanting to do that all day. You have no idea."

Julia sat next to Ruth and took her hand. Julian stayed by the entrance.

"Where were you?" Julia said.

"At work. I'm preparing for a trial."

"Domestic violence?" Julia squinted.

"Yes, and you know how I feel about those cases." Ruth spread her arms. "So give me a hug."

He watched mother and daughter embrace. Julia needed this.

"Remember what I used to say when I was little?"

"Hold me forever?" Ruth stroked Julia's hair.

She nodded and sniffled.

Ruth put her hands on Julia's waist. "You've lost weight. Are you dieting?"

"I don't eat, because of the nausea."

"From the headaches?" Ruth covered her mouth.

Julia nodded. "I'm seeing a neurologist tomorrow. He's Julian's college roommate. Mom . . . I think this is serious."

"Well, I'm keeping my hopes up." Ruth stood and adjusted her dress. "But whatever happens, just know I'll be there for you."

"I never doubted that." Julia almost cried.

"You're staying over, aren't you?" Ruth's gaze went from Julia to Julian.

Julia looked at him. He nodded.

"I've just redone the guest bedroom," Ruth said. "You'll be comfortable there."

"If you don't mind," Julia said, "we'd like to stay in my room."

"But the bed is so small." Ruth held up two fingers barely apart.

"We'll manage." Julia put her arm around Julian.

"You want memories," Ruth said

"You know me."

———

They made love on the canopy bed. It was quick but passionate. They were good at taking advantage of brief moments together and often found themselves in the same mood romantically. Thankfully, their room was the farthest from Ruth's. They'd been quiet until Julia cried out as she came. He kissed her mouth to squelch it. Now she rocked with her knees against her chest.

"You were a happy child?" He moved a strand of her hair away from her face.

"My father died when I was six. That wasn't easy. Still, there were good times. It was just the three of us. If my mom felt sorry for herself, she never showed it. She always tried to make us happy. Even when Dina and I didn't make it easy for her . . . I'll never forget that."

He pictured a young Julia and her sister on opposite ends of the couch. The soles of their feet press together as Julia reads a mystery, Dina a cookbook.

"Did you and your sister always get along?"

"We had our share of fights. But we never stayed mad at each other for more than a day. She was my best friend when I was growing up, even though she was older."

He traced his fingers over the dip at her waist, the rise of her hip.

"That feels wonderful." She lay on her stomach and closed her eyes. Her breaths grew shallow—she must have dozed off.

His fingertips continued roaming her skin. He fell into a light trance.

Remember—

Her car is in front of her building. He puts his hand on its hood. It's warm. He's called her at home and work and on her cell. No answer. He holds the door for a dog and his master as they leave the building. No need to get buzzed in. He passes the elevator, climbs the stairs two at a time. Three flights later he's in front of 3D, panting. He turns the doorknob. It's unlocked. He goes in—

"My mother—" Julia shook him gently. "Hon, are you okay?"

"Fine, I just . . . What were you saying?"

"My mother looked a little tired."

"She did." He lay on his back. "Maybe she just needs some rest. Let's see how she is in the morning."

Her head found his chest. He stared at the ceiling as she held him.

"Julia." He tried to get a look at her but couldn't when she held him tighter "When did you *first* see me that night?"

There was a pause.

"At the hospital," she whispered.

———

Julian dreamed a black knight with a lance in hand is riding toward him. He steps aside. The lance sticks in the wall and vibrates like a tuning fork. The knight jumps off his horse and flips up his visor. It's Richard. Julian runs up the stairs and tiptoes toward a bedroom in darkness. He hears a cry. Is it pain or pleasure? Elevator doors in front of him. He pushes a button. The doors part. He steps into the cab and starts to fall. He can't scream.

"Hon . . . hon!" Julia was shaking him.

He opened his eyes.

"You were having a nightmare."

He shook cobwebs out of his head.

"I'm okay," he said. "How are you?"

"The pain is really bad. Maybe some pressure can give me some relief?"

"How?"

"Squeeze my temples as hard as you can. It might help."

"You mean like this?" He put his thumb and forefinger on either side of her head and felt the indentation.

"Right there, but harder. Go on."

He squeezed hard until the tip of his thumb turned white.

"You can make it harder than that."

He did.

"Oh yes," she said after a couple of minutes. "That feels so good. Just hold it."

Another minute passed. His fingers ached, the tips numb.

"Okay . . . you can stop now," she said.

He let go and shook out his hand.

"Thank you." She kissed him and then fell back on the mattress. Her eyes were half-closed. She was sick—but with what? And how bad was it?

"Take anything?" he said.

"Everything." Her voice was almost too quiet to hear. "Nothing helps."

CHAPTER 15

Julian and Julia walked the city streets to Nelson Ruble's office, holding hands.

"It's wonderful down here." She was looking around as she kept up with his steady pace.

"It is." He watched people dart all around them. There was an Indian restaurant next to an electronics store with a middle-aged man out front telling passersby he had great deals on all the latest gadgets. They passed a crowded trattoria with outdoor tables, the scent of marinara lingering in the air.

"Could you live down here?" Julia said.

"Absolutely." He imagined them renting an apartment, going to indie movies, off-Broadway plays, art galleries. Sitting in outdoor cafes and watching people. At night, they'd walk until they found yet another eclectic place to eat.

Julian recalled Nelson in their dorm room, hunched over a textbook. Back then Nellie had long hair and a pimply face and was fascinated by brains. Was that kid now the man who could save Julia?

———

"Julian." Nelson hugged him. "And Julia."

She and the doctor shook hands.

"Whatever's going on, I'll do everything I can to help you."

"I know you will," Julia said.

Nellie sat behind his desk. Julian and Julia had taken the two chairs in front of it.

"I was just reviewing your intake questionnaire," Nelson said as he looked at his computer monitor. "Your grandfather died of a brain tumor?"

"Grandpa Leo. He was on my father's side." Julia lurched forward. "Is that bad?"

"Not unless we're talking about several family members, which I'm assuming *isn't* the case in your situation?"

"That's right." She sounded confident. Julian relaxed a bit.

"Your headaches have become more frequent and severe?" Nelson said.

She nodded.

"There's also been some trouble seeing?" Nelson looked away from the monitor.

"Yes, a blind spot." Her tone was unsteady. "That just started."

Julian put his arm around her. She leaned into him.

The nurse poked her head in. "Doctor, you should have access to the visual field exam now," she said.

"Thanks." Nellie started typing. "Got it."

The nurse left, closing the door behind her.

Nellie stared at the screen, eyes flicking back and forth. Then he looked up at them. "We need to start ruling things out," he said.

"Could it be a tumor?" Julia moved to the edge of her seat.

"I'm not saying it is." Nelson clasped his hands in front of him.

"But it could be?" she said.

"Yes, it's possible."

Tears were in her eyes.

"We need to run more tests," Nelson said. "I'll expedite everything and get them done today."

"Today?" Julia said.

"I wouldn't wait."

"Maybe . . . we should get it done while we're here," Julian said. "Might be more efficient in the long run."

"Fine." She sighed. "Let's get it over with."

———

He held Julia's hand as they stepped past two parting glass doors. As soon as the pine scent hit him, he remembered lying in a hospital bed, leg raised in a cast. His skin crawled. He hadn't wanted to be back in a hospital so soon.

A guard directed them to the second floor, where Julia would have a series of tests. They walked along a hallway. A woman on a gurney sped past them from the opposite direction. About Julia's age, thin with dark hair. A nurse and a doctor were on either side of her, jogging. Her eyes were closed. Julia picked up her pace. So did Julian.

"The thought of being put to sleep gives me the creeps." She squeezed his hand. "I'm afraid I'll never wake up."

He squeezed back. "Will you be okay?" he said.

"As long as you're with me."

"I will be."

———

They were led straight into Nellie's office the next day. Julian looked over at Julia in her chair. She had dark circles under her eyes and her hair was mussed. She'd said she spent the night staring at the ceiling.

"Julia," Nellie said. "I've got the results back from all your tests . . . Unfortunately, there's a problem."

Julia grabbed Julian's hand and clutched it tight.

There were three light boxes to the left of Nellie's desk. He removed two scans from a big envelope and snapped them in place. He flipped a switch and the images lit up, each showing the two hemispheres of Julia's brain.

"This is a tumor." He pointed to a small mass on the first image with the tip of his pen. "It's on the frontal lobe." He faced them. "I've spoken to the best neurosurgeon I know. I'd like you to meet with him this afternoon."

———

A few hours later they were sitting in Dr. Rig's office on two leather club chairs. On the small table between them was a bowl filled with candy. *Dark Chocolate = Brain Food* was printed on each red wrapper.

Rig was seated behind a big oak desk. He was handsome, early forties with a weathered look. He was trim and had a full head of brown hair.

"I've had an extensive discussion with Dr. Ruble and Dr. Weston Ford, who also specializes in these types of conditions," Rig said. "The three of us concur. Surgery is the solution."

"How soon?" Julia held her temples.

"The sooner we operate the better," Rig said.

"Doctor," Julia said, "I need some time to mentally prepare for this."

"Ms. Rodgers, I'm very good at what I do. Dr. Ruble is a colleague and a friend, and I will do everything I can to cure you, but I'm afraid we don't have much time."

Julian flinched. What would Alan Wright do?

"We can expedite the pre-op tests." Rig tapped the tablet screen with his stylus. "How's tomorrow afternoon?"

There was a moment of silence. Julian was about to speak when Julia's chest rose.

"Okay." Her face was white. "I'll be ready."

———

Julian was driving north on the thruway. He was in the center lane.

"I'm sure Rig knows what he's doing," Julia said. "He sounded confident. I liked that about him." Her lower lip trembled. "The tumor is bad enough, but they're going to put me to sleep. What happens if I don't wake up?"

"Hon, I wish it were me and not you."

"You're sweet."

"But of course you'll wake up. You do know that, don't you?"

"I'm just scared."

He eyed the speedometer. He was impressed with Rig, but everyone said Alan Wright was brilliant, the very best—and Julia deserved the very best.

"As soon as you're better, we're going back to a villa in Jamaica." He put on his blinker and got into the right lane.

"If I get better."

"Shush." He slowed the vehicle as he pulled onto the exit ramp. He imagined her on the operating table. A surgeon and his assistants surround her. She sleeps even though bright lights shine on her. The anesthesiologist sits next to her head, monitoring her vitals as he keeps her unconscious—

"Have I had this since I was a little girl?" she said. "Or is it recent . . . punishment for something I've done?"

"It's not your fault. You must know that."

Remember—

He's going down the hallway. He reaches a door. It's open. He looks in and sees a woman's back. Long dark hair flows down—

A horn honked. The light ahead of him was green. He made his way through the intersection, shaken.

"I really *am* sorry for my existential crisis." She put her hand on his thigh. "It cost us time when we could've been happy. I want to make it up to you."

Words he'd longed to hear. But now Julia was sick, and her tumor might be malignant—might even have metastasized. And if he was the one who ran the light, he'd be incarcerated.

How much time did they really have left?

———

Julian stood by the door of Julia's hospital room.

Ruth was on the bed, lying alongside Julia, who was curled up tight. She often was when in pain. She said it seemed to help.

"When you were six," Ruth said, "you had to get a tooth pulled. The dentist sat you in his chair. You were shaking. He pulled the tooth and your face turned white, but you were determined not to cry."

"I pretended the dentist's light was the sun and I was on a beach," Julia said.

"Sometimes I've been overwhelmed, about to give up," Ruth said. "Then I'd think about that expression on your face and knew I couldn't. But now I feel so helpless."

"Don't worry, Mom. I've got a good feeling about things."

Ruth lowered her eyes. They both knew Julia was lying.

———

Julian stepped into the hall outside Julia's hospital room and took out his cell. There were three missed calls and a message from Slattery. Julian was debating whether he should call back when the phone vibrated. He answered it.

"You're a hard man to get in touch with," Slattery said.

"Julia has a brain tumor."

"Sorry to hear that." He paused. "You know, the best neurosurgeon around could be wrongly accused of a crime he didn't commit—unless you remembered something?"

"You don't beat around the bush."

"Subtlety isn't one of my finer attributes."

Julian walked in a circle. "To answer your question, I still don't remember."

"Imagine Cheryl's parents at the morgue," Slattery said. "The pain they must've felt when they saw her lying there." There was crackling on the line. "They'll never get over that."

"I'm sorry for them, but you still don't know it's my fault."

"Alan Wright shouldn't have to bear the weight of guilt if it's not his." Again Slattery paused. "I hope Julia recovers soon." He hung up.

Julian put his phone away, took a step, and saw Evelyn Wright going down the hall perpendicular to him. His pulse spiked, then eased when she continued on, not noticing him. Moments later he saw Melvin headed in the same direction.

Julian waited another minute before returning to Julia's room.

———

Julian's heart palpitated and his teeth were numb. Coffee—he'd had too much of it. Julia was in the operating room. He watched the door and imagined Dr. Rig barging through it, smiling. *I got all of it.* Or he could enter gloomily and say, *I can't help her.* Julian had played each scenario out in his head a dozen times, preparing for the worst and hoping for the best. Ruth's eyes were half-closed as she sat in the corner absent-mindedly flipping pages in a magazine. Dina and Reed sat next to her.

"The cafeteria is closing soon," Julian said. "I'm getting something to eat. Does anybody want anything?"

Just then Rig barged into the waiting room. He pulled off his surgical mask.

"We got most of it," he said. "But not all."

"So she isn't cured?" Julian said. His second-worst fear realized.

"Not yet," Rig said. "But now I know what I'm dealing with."

Wright would have gotten it all.

"Doctor." Ruth stepped in front of Julian. "When can she go home?"

"In a couple of days, with no complications. She takes it easy for a week and can resume normal activity after that. She should see some relief in the short term. In the meantime, I've got to come up with a game plan."

———

A beeping sound came from the room next door. It was the intravenous machine. Julian knew this because Julia had one hooked up to her. The alarm had been on for a minute when someone shouted that she'd take care of it. Ruth sat in the chair next to Julia's bed. Her eyes were red and she sniffled intermittently.

"The replacement part is cheap," Julia said. "Getting to it is the bitch."

"What was that, baby?" Ruth said.

"My mechanic's response as to why it cost three hundred to change a dashboard bulb."

Ruth smiled sadly.

"Mom, remember when we shopped for my prom dress?"

"You didn't want to go." Ruth dabbed her eyes with a tissue.

"That's putting it mildly." Julia turned to Julian. "I locked myself in my room so no one would see my pimples. I was lean, strong, and athletic. My breasts were developing just fine and I had great hair. But I only saw the acne." She pouted. "Mostly on my cheeks."

"We'd been in a standoff." Ruth shoved a thumb at Julia. "She can be stubborn, this one."

"I wasn't going shopping for a prom dress and that was that," Julia said. "Then Mom yells, 'Stand back!' and kicks open my bedroom door."

"You left me no choice."

"Mom, I put on that dress, looked in the mirror, and saw what I had. That changed me."

"I wonder if I should've pushed you more." Ruth pursed her lips. "If there were other things you would've done if I had."

"You did it just right." She reached for her mother's hand.

After a moment, Ruth rose. "I'll give you two some time together." She patted Julian's shoulder on her way out.

Once they were alone, he bent down and let his lips linger on Julia's.

"The rest of the world disappears when you do that." She shut her eyes. "It's just us, being with each other. Remember that first day in Jamaica? There was so much promise then."

He pictured her lying on that beach, her graceful body, perfectly proportioned. His fingers gliding on her glistening skin.

"Julian, there's something I need to tell you."

His stomach tumbled.

"I love your green eyes," she said.

"That's it?" His muscles relaxed a bit.

"That night . . ." she said as if they'd already been talking about it.

"The night of the accident?"

"Yes." She looked down. His heart accelerated.

"You were with Richard?"

"Julian, I was never going to see him again. I—"

"You cheated on me?" Tears streamed down his cheeks. He didn't wipe them. They kept falling. She put her hand on his and he pulled away.

"We didn't—"

"Don't." He held up his hands. "You kissed him? Let him touch you?"

"Yes . . . but—"

Her eyes brimmed with tears. His were filling up, too.

"I wish you hadn't told me." He hadn't meant to say it out loud.

"I just wanted you to hear it from me."

CHAPTER 16

Julian stood outside in front of two thick glass doors, taking deep breaths to calm himself. Inside, an attractive receptionist beckoned him. He pulled the door open and stepped in.

"Can I help you?" *Linda Jenks* was on her nameplate.

"I'm here for the deposition." He adjusted his tie. "Julian Barnes."

Linda looked at a clipboard and ran an index finger down it.

"Did you park in the lot on Backus?" she said.

"As per the directions." His leg was shaking.

"I'll validate your ticket." Linda stuck out her hand.

"Thanks." He handed her the receipt.

She stamped it and returned it to him.

"Please come with me."

He noticed her bright red high heels and perfect posture as he followed her down a long hallway. The carpet was thick, the air conditioner on high. Linda stopped in front of an open door.

"There's a continental breakfast inside and the restroom is across the hall." She raised her eyebrows. "Anything else?"

"No, thanks."

She smiled and left.

He stepped into the room. Everyone was seated around an oblong table. The men all wore ties—now he was glad he'd decided to wear one even though ties irritated his neck.

Wright was dressed impeccably in a gray suit. The court reporter was in his shirt sleeves, jacket hanging on the back of his chair, tie tight. He had red hair and was probably nearing thirty. Julian's stomach knotted as he sat between him and the man next to Wright.

"I'm Brian Marks." He was clean-cut and handsome, and his navy suit fit him to a T. "I represent Dr. Wright."

A heavyset man in a three-piece alabaster suit sat across from him. He leaned forward. "I'm Burl Sutton." He had white hair and a matching beard. "These are my clients, Mr. and Mrs. Star, the parents of Cheryl Star." Mr. Star was middle-aged with a wide girth and thick bags under his eyes. His wife was his size and age and had an attractive face that was still very pretty and brown hair that ended at the shoulders of her black dress.

"Hello." Julian made brief eye contact with each of them.

"It's after ten." Burl tapped his watch.

"Evelyn isn't here yet," Wright said.

"We'll have to begin without her." Brian didn't seem disappointed. "Ready, Julian?"

"Yes." He was about to get up when Brian put his hand on his shoulder.

"You can stay there."

He sat back down. The court reporter swore him in.

"Julian," Brian said, "we know there are parts of the night of October 2, 2009, that you *don't* remember. Let's begin with you telling us what you *do* from, say, six in the evening on?"

"I'd bought tickets to *Phantom of the Opera*." His heels dug into the carpet. "I was home, preparing to go to my girlfriend's . . . to surprise her." The vision of Julia's back popped into his mind again. Now he understood where it came from, though he still didn't remember.

"Do you remember getting into your car?" Brian said.

"Yes." He went back to the moment. He is sitting in the driver's seat, hands on the wheel. "I recall the dashboard clock reading 7:30 p.m. That means I would have arrived by eight."

Don't remember.

"So you made it to your girlfriend's house?" Brian slid his hands into his pockets.

"My girlfriend lives in an apartment." He wiped sweat from his upper lip.

"Do you recall making it there?"

Julian ran his finger under his shirt collar. This was it. He couldn't lie. He would have to tell the truth and deal with the consequences. He was about to speak when the door opened.

Linda stuck her head in and beckoned Brian. "I need to talk to you."

His face darkened. "Excuse me." He left and returned a few moments later. "Alan, could you please come with us?"

"Is it Eve?" Wright rose.

"No," Brian said. "Please step outside for a minute."

Wright walked out the door, which Marks closed behind them.

———

"The district attorney has just brought formal charges against Dr. Wright," Brian said when he and Wright were back in the room. "Burl, I'd appreciate some time to confer with my client, given these new circumstances."

Two questions bounced around in Julian's head. Was there new evidence? Did it exonerate him?

Wright clutched the back of a chair. Trisha Star was staring at him.

"We forgive you," she said.

"I knew you could say it." Mr. Star hugged his wife, and she fell into him.

Wright hung his head.

Julian saw Julia lying in the hospital room. She'd cheated on him. That made him angry. She could die. That made him so sad he didn't think he could bear it.

"You *still* don't remember, do you?" Wright said.

Julian shook his head.

"We need to settle," Wright said.

"Alan." Brian held up a hand. "We *must* discuss this in private."

"Settle," Wright said. "It's best for everyone." His arm swept the air. "These proceedings will take a toll on all of us."

"I agree," Trisha said.

Wright gave the Stars a pleading look. "I was going to ask her to marry me."

"Dr. Wright, are you serious about settling?" Burl said.

"Yes." Wright looked toward the floor. "Would you accept five million dollars? I know money can't make up for your loss, but it's all I—"

"What are you doing?" Brian grabbed Wright's bicep.

"I've listened to you enough." Wright shook himself free. "Draw up the documents."

Trisha Star's hands were trembling. Her husband had his arm around her.

"Alan, you're making the district attorney's case," Brian said.

"We're not admitting guilt—that must be clear. I didn't run that light."

"What's going on?" Evelyn Wright stood in the doorway. She wore a green dress, her blond hair in a chignon.

Silence filled the room.

"The district attorney," Brian said, "just sent an e-mail to all concerned parties stating that based on new evidence regarding Dr. Wright's health, they are charging him with sec-ond-degree vehicular manslaughter."

"What health issues?" Burl said.

"I'm not aware of any." Brian locked his briefcase. "The DA said specifics would be forthcoming."

"That's absurd." Evelyn put her hand on Wright's shoulder. "You're not responsible. I know it for a fact."

Burl and Brian looked at each other.

"Eve, she died while she was with me." Wright's chest rose. "I loved her. I've got to do something."

"Mr. and Mrs. Star are aware Dr. Wright had feelings for their daughter," Burl said.

"We need to understand what's behind this false accusation." Evelyn slipped her arm around Wright.

"I understand, but it doesn't change how I feel," Wright said. "I need to settle."

"I'm confused." Evelyn's eyes were questioning. "Do you want my *permission*?"

"I want your support!" Wright held up his fists. "Why do you make everything so difficult?"

"Alan, no one stops you from getting what you want," Evelyn said. "Brian, please draw up the necessary papers. If this is what he wants, we'll do as Alan wishes."

CHAPTER 17

I just wanted you to hear it from me.

Julian crossed Sunrise's parking lot, gait even. Inside, he ached. When he reached his car he came to a halt.

Slattery, wearing a gray trench coat and smoking a cigar, was leaning on the door.

Julian's pulse quickened as he met Slattery's steely gaze. "You came here looking for me?"

"Just got lucky." Slattery patted his breast pocket. "Had to see my cardiologist."

"Hope it's not serious." He was sincere. The man was a nuisance, but Julian didn't dislike him, much less wish him off this earth.

"Actually it was good news."

Brring, brring. It sounded like an old-fashioned telephone. Slattery unclipped his cell. *Brring, brring.*

"I'll deal with this later." He silenced it. "Right now we've got something more important to do."

"*We?*"

"Yeah. Let's go for a ride."

"Where?"

"You know. Don't tell me you haven't tried?"

Julian had managed to avoid going down Wendt toward Brewster. What had happened at Julia's had to be related to the accident, but he couldn't be sure until he remembered. Was Julia right about its being better if he didn't? It'd keep Cough at bay, too.

No. If he caused the accident, he had to know. He did, after all, have to live with himself.

"I've tried other things." Julian felt his jaw tighten. "Just not this."

"Then I'd say it's about time." Slattery had his chin raised. Big cleft in it. "If it works, you find out right away. If not, we say we tried and leave it at that."

"I don't think so."

"Alan Wright is accused of killing the woman he loved. How would you feel if someone accused you of killing Julia?"

"What are you talking about?" His hands formed fists. "Who would do that?"

"I'm just giving you an example." Slattery appeared to study him. "If you remember, you'll feel like yourself again."

Don't remember.

"Come on," Slattery said. "Let's go."

"You're relentless." He unlocked his vehicle. They both got

in. He started the ignition, put his hand on the shift, and directed the stick until the *D* lit.

"Let's go to Julia's to get the same starting point." Slattery opened his window.

Julian checked his surroundings and then slowly pulled out of the space. He gazed at his rearview mirror. The imaginary police cruiser was there, following him, waiting to ticket him for any infraction. No margin of error. His hands were on the wheel at nine and three—the latest traffic-safety recommendation. He came to a full stop when specified and rolled forward afterward to ensure it was safe before proceeding through the intersection. He yielded the right of way when required and halted for red lights, always applying the brake when the light turned yellow. Now his car chugged up a steep entrance ramp. At the top, he put on his blinker and checked his side mirror. No one. His foot pushed the gas pedal until the vehicle settled in the right lane at fifty-five. A car was in the distance, no more than a dot. He flicked on his blinker again and turned the wheel until he was in the center lane.

"You certainly are a careful driver," Slattery said. "I give you that."

"I pretend police are following me. I've been doing it since the first time I got behind the wheel." Julian exited the parkway, made a turn at the end of the ramp, and drove along tree-lined suburban streets.

Now Julia's building was just ahead.

I just wanted you to hear it from me.

"Where did you park that night?" Slattery said.

"Up the block."

"Pull over there."

He eased off the gas and steered right. A red truck was in the space he'd been in. He double-parked next to it.

They sat for a while in silence. Nothing happened. Julian didn't feel a thing except a modicum of relief.

"Okay." Slattery took out a cigar and removed the cellophane wrapper. "Go down the hill and we'll call it a day."

Julian inhaled the scent of fresh tobacco as he put the car into gear. Wendt had tall trees and slate sidewalks. The houses were raised ranches, set back a bit, each a neutral color. They crossed Cunningham and continued up until they reached the top. He stomped on the brake and stared down at Brewster below.

"You've come this far," Slattery said. "You can't stop."

Remember—

He's going down a hill.

Now he removed his foot from the brake and the car rolled down Wendt toward Brewster, accelerating because of the grade. He pressed the pedal to keep the speed just below the limit. Wind whipped in from Slattery's open window.

Remember—

He can't.

"You saw something in her apartment." Slattery spoke like he had the answer. "That put you over the edge. Your being such a careful driver just proves it was something big, something important."

Slattery was right.

"I *don't* remember." Though now he had a pretty good idea of what he saw.

"I believe you." Slattery ran his unlit cigar under his nose.

"I'm done for today." He began braking. "This isn't helping, at least not me."

Slattery didn't react.

Julian turned on his blinker and pulled over. He put the car in "park" and took in a deep breath.

"You okay?" Slattery peered at him.

"Fine." Julian swallowed hard.

"I appreciate you trying. That tells me something about you."

"I don't trust people easily, Slattery, but I'm going to trust you."

"I'm listening."

"Someone doesn't want me to remember what happened that night."

"Who?"

"I don't know his name. But he threatened to kill Julia if I do."

Slattery jerked upright.

"Now we're getting somewhere." He produced a pad and pencil. "Can you describe him?"

"I never got a good look at his face. All I can tell you is his mouth is a grim line and he has salt-and-pepper hair. He's round, I'd say early fifties, with a limp and he coughs."

"Coughs?"

"A lot. Like it's a habit, maybe a reflex."

Slattery scribbled something down. "Sounds like someone has a serious beef with Alan Wright."

"Could it be a patient?"

"Alan's never had a malpractice case."

"That doesn't rule out the possibility."

"No, but it does makes it tough to investigate."

"What about business dealings?"

"None that I know of." Slattery held up his pad. "I'll check with the police, see if they have anything on anyone matching this limited description. But without a name that's a long shot."

"What can I do?"

"You already did all you can by telling me." Slattery laid a hand on his shoulder. "Now sit tight. I'll take it from here."

CHAPTER 18

Julian was running at a steady pace, halfway through his goal of three miles. His heart pounded. Blood pressure and pulse perked. Lungs took in the big breaths needed to work his arms and legs, until his muscles tired and his mind cleared. Exerting himself to the point of exhaustion, too tired to feel or think, had often been an effective remedy for emotional pain. He'd given up running when he first met Julia, as she had her yoga classes—sacrifices to give them more time together.

He came to a corner and jogged in place while a car passed. He'd stopped running to gain more time with the woman he loved. Now he was running to purge the pain she'd caused him.

His sneaker pushed off the curb as he made a right and went up Holland heading toward Adee. He wasn't far from home. Three miles in twenty-eight minutes was good enough for him. He put on one last burst of speed. *She kissed him.* He couldn't even get past that.

His lungs were starved for air. Wind came at him as he stretched out his legs until his muscles resisted. He passed his imaginary finish line and sometime after slowed to a walk. Then he stopped, leaned over, held his knees, and caught his breath, sweating freely, pores spilling toxins as endorphins flooded his brain.

Could he forgive her?

No—not while the movie of her with Richard was still running in his head. How could she? He could never do that to her, not in a million years.

He sat on a curb. Watching reruns of Julia with Richard wasn't doing him any good. He had an idea—at least it would distract him.

———

The stoplight analysis was still in his suitcase. He hadn't opened it since coming back from Jamaica. He'd had a lot on his mind then, too much to study it the way he should have. Now he'd take another look.

Julian opened the binder. It had a summary page on top, and the ones behind it drilled down into the details. It was impressive, at least in presentation. The first tab had a two-page narrative that explained the basis of the calculations. He read through that along with the rest of the material.

The data was gathered over a ten-day period in February—a single-digit cold snap. The accident had occurred on a balmy October night. Temperature could affect the timing mechanism—that was in the assumptions.

It was also documented that the light had been repaired in December. Had Slattery read this? Unlikely—he'd probably just seen the top number and run with it.

Julian grabbed the mouse and the screen saver of swimming fish dissolved. He opened the browser and typed *Alan Wright* into Google's window. He scrolled through the results and saw a link to an article about a grant the doctor's foundation had made to the children's wing of Sunrise Hospital— Evelyn Wright was administering it. Another link described a new technique Wright had developed. Once refined, it could save hundreds, perhaps thousands, of lives. The oldest article was about growing up in a family of neurosurgeons.

He wasn't sure what he was looking for, but this wasn't it. He closed the browser and pushed his chair away from the desk.

———

Julian showed the guard at Sunrise a check for two thousand dollars, payable to Wright's foundation.

"I'd like to give it to Miss Wright personally," he said.

The guard picked up a handset. "What's your name?"

"Julian Barnes." He figured Evelyn's curiosity would get the better of her. The guard turned away and spoke quietly into the handset. After a moment he turned back to Julian.

"She's on the third floor. Follow the signs to 315."

When he got there, Evelyn was by the door. "I must say, this is a surprise, Mr. Barnes." She leaned against the jamb.

"Thanks for seeing me on such short notice."

She held out her arm to usher him in.

"Hopefully, it's good news." Evelyn's office contained few clues as to who occupied it other than her pharmaceutical diploma and a photo on the desk depicting her and Wright as teenagers. She closed the door and sat on a couch across from him. Her perfume was so captivating he found himself drawing in one deep breath after another.

"Are you turning yourself in?" She tugged her skirt down over her knees.

"No. I still haven't remembered, but the question is, why would someone want me *not* to?" He stared at her, looking for a clue.

She cocked her head. "I'm confused."

"Someone made a serious threat against me—well, someone close to me—if I remember." He'd give her enough to intrigue her.

Now she was frowning. "That's quite bizarre."

"This wasn't a note or a phone call, either." Recalling the pain he'd felt when Cough dug his knuckles into his ribs, he rubbed his side. "It was physical."

"Do you know the name of this brute of a man?"

"How did you know it was a man?"

"I mean . . . I'm assuming he must've been to inflict such physical pain." She paused. "So again, Mr. Barnes . . . do you know his name?"

"No."

"Could you give a facial description?"

"His mouth was straight, rather expressionless, and he has

salt-and-pepper hair." Julian shrugged. "I never got a good look at him."

"I'm sorry to hear about what happened," she said. "But with so little to go on there isn't much I can do. You could go to the police, but I doubt they'll be much help."

"I would have thought someone with your extensive rcsources—"

"Without more details, I'm afraid not." She wrinkled her forehead. "We want you to remember. I think that's been made clear."

"Maybe this individual has a vendetta against Alan?"

"Mr. Barnes, do you realize who we're talking about?"

"There must be someone," he said. "A disgruntled patient?"

"He's never had a malpractice suit brought against him."

"I'm just trying to find the truth."

"Then you're looking in the wrong place." Evelyn tapped her temple. "The answer is in your head. The sooner you remember, the better it will be . . . for all of us."

She wasn't helping him—but there was someone else in Sunrise he could talk to. He tried to appear thoughtful.

"I'm sorry to have bothered you." He reached into his jacket pocket and removed the check. "Here's my donation." He handed it to her. "It's from my personal funds."

"I appreciate this." She glanced at the check.

"Have a good day, Ms. Wright."

He stepped toward the entrance and she moved to follow him.

"I hope you remember soon." She closed the door behind him.

He went to the end of the hall and took the stairs down one landing to the second floor. It looked familiar. There were two nurses at the station, chatting. He didn't know either of them. One was male, and as Julian approached, he looked up.

"Can I help you?" he said.

"I was looking for Leah."

"She's not here." His name tag said *Derek*.

"Do you know when she will be?" Julian tried to sound polite.

Derek wrinkled his brow. "Who are you?"

"My name is Julian Barnes. I was a patient here and just wanted to thank her for taking such good care of me."

"I'll let her know." Derek was already turning back toward the other nurse.

"I was hoping to do it in person." Julian stepped closer to their workstation.

Derek shook his head. "I'm not allowed to give out someone's schedule."

"Okay. Thanks for your help." Julian turned and walked away, having just recalled Leah's schedule from when he was a patient there.

———

He arrived at Sunrise the next day and pulled into the indoor lot, past the row of reserved spots. A luxury sports car filled the first one, *Evelyn* on the license plate.

He went up to the next level, parked, and walked toward the elevators. The sound of his heels echoed off the walls. He took the elevator to the second floor, got off, and turned right down a wide hallway with doors on both sides.

Melvin was buffing the floors. He and Julian exchanged a nod. Julian reached the nurse's station and found Leah there, alone.

"Can I help you?" Her mouth was a straight line as he stood in front of her desk.

"Leah, it's me, Julian. I was a patient in here last fall. You gave me excellent care." He took a step forward. "Do you remember me?"

"Why, yes. Did you leave something? Nothing was turned into Lost and Found . . . that I know of."

Melvin passed them, his buffer leading the way. Julian waited until he was out of earshot.

"Leah, I'm trying to help Dr. Wright."

She looked confused. "How?" she said.

"Someone seems have a vendetta against him. They've threatened me." He was taking a chance by revealing this after his meeting with Evelyn, but he had to start trusting people or he'd never get anywhere. "Maybe a patient, someone he operated on?"

Her expression made it clear that she wasn't going to tell him anything. Maybe Cough had threatened her, too? Having firsthand experience of that, he wasn't going to make things any more difficult for her than they might already be.

"Sorry to have bothered you." He walked backward, facing

her with his hands in his pockets. Then he turned and picked up his pace as he made his way back toward the elevators, the sound of the buffer getting louder.

"You're looking for the wrong thing," Melvin said.

"Excuse me?"

Melvin shut off the buffer and glanced around. No one was in sight.

"It's not who he operated on," he said. "It's who he *didn't*."

"What are you talking about?"

"I heard you ask Leah about Dr. Wright," Melvin said. "Been here five years. Happened one of my first days on the job. It was May."

Julian watched the elevator doors close. A nurse came walking toward them, her big eyes roaming. She was tall and blond.

"She's going to take the elevator down," Melvin said under his breath. "Get on with her. I'll meet you in the lobby in ten minutes."

"Got it."

The nurse stopped when she came to the bank of elevators, pushed the "down" button, and stepped back.

"Hello, Melvin," she said.

"Hi, Joyce."

"You're on until ten?"

"Yep."

"I can sign your timecard," she said.

Melvin thanked her as the elevator came to their floor. Joyce got out on the second floor, Julian at the lobby. There was a coffee shop and, in front of a service desk, a row of chairs. He sat in one. A big clock on the wall ahead of him showed 8 p.m.

At 8:10, he looked around for Melvin. There were only two other people in the waiting area. That's when he saw Evelyn Wright coming toward him.

"Excuse me, are you waiting for Mr. Winters?" She spoke as if she'd never met him.

Julian did his best to look perplexed.

"Melvin Winters?" She raised her eyebrows. "You were questioning him?"

"The man in maintenance?"

"That's him."

"I wasn't questioning him. I was—"

"No need to explain." Evelyn held up a hand. "Melvin said to tell you he can't make it and you should go."

"And he chose you to be his messenger?"

"I think it's best if you leave, Mr. Barnes." Her eyes went toward the door. "And please don't come back here unless you need medical attention." She gave him a narrow look. "And even then, you might want to consider another hospital."

"I'll leave." He glared at her. "But you've got me all wrong, Ms. Wright. I'm trying to help your brother." He turned and walked away.

———

Julian stood on the sidewalk across the street from Sunrise Hospital. It was a little after ten. He was glad he had worn a windbreaker. If he smoked, he'd be having a cigarette, ready to toss it at a moment's notice.

A man emerged from the service entrance of Sunrise. Julian walked up to him.

"Melvin," he said.

"Get away from me." Melvin picked up his gait.

Julian kept pace. "I need to talk to you."

"No way." Melvin went faster. "I could lose my job—I can't afford that." He had fear in his eyes. "Besides, I've already told you enough. You just need to do a little digging on your own." He pointed to the hospital with a thumb. "It's in there. Check the records."

Then he took off.

———

Julian got into his car the following morning. The dashboard clock read 11:11 a.m. He imagined that Julia was in the seat next to him, wearing the short red polka-dot dress she'd worn on their first date. She leans against the passenger door, her feet in his lap. Her pink painted toes playfully poke his thigh while she shows him plenty of hers. She smiles and says, *Don't worry, hon. It's going to be all right.*

Which it would be, if only Alan Wright—

"Good morning, Mr. Barnes." A gravelly voice from behind him.

He was about to turn around when he felt a hand on the back of his neck.

"No moving." Cough. "And keep your eyes away from the mirror."

Julian dropped his eyes to the wheel.

Cough let go of his neck. "Julia Rodgers is an easy target."

"What did you do to her?" His insides cringed.

"Nothing yet."

Julian risked a glance at the rearview mirror. He saw a dark cap and salt–and-pepper hair.

Cough smacked the back of his head. "Eyes away from the mirror."

Julian stared at his lap.

"You were snooping around the hospital," Cough said. "Asking questions about Wright."

"What makes you think—"

"I told you I'd be listening." Cough. "Don't undermine my plans." His breath was warm on the back of Julian's neck. "You know what I want, right?"

"That I don't remember. Which I haven't."

"Good. Now put your head down and don't pick it up until you count to fifty, got it?"

"One, two, three . . ."

CHAPTER 19

An electronic voice told Julian to go right at the end of the block. He made the turn and then switched off the navigation system—it had been a while, but he knew how to get there.

Half an hour later, he exited the thruway and drove along a two-lane road. On his left, fields stretched to the horizon. Cows grazed, horses looked over fences. Barns and silos dotted the distance. He slowed and made a right, then another into Tom's driveway. The road narrowed. There was no shoulder, but there was a creek. The road's pavement ran out and pebbles sprayed the car's underside. He'd go for the undercarriage cleaning next time he was at the carwash.

The long driveway was so rocky the car shimmied. It was like riding on the moon. Tom talked about paving it but still hadn't gotten around to it. He'd say that if anyone robbed him, at least they'd have a hell of a time getting away.

Julian finally came to the small cabin tucked between two

trees. Behind the stream that ran past it was a mountain the two of them had once climbed all the way to the top. He pulled in next to a red pickup, put his car in "park," and got out.

Tom was sitting on his front porch with a leg up on the banister, holding a beer. Rebel, his golden retriever, was stretched out on the floor next to him.

"We've got to get the money out of politics." Tom stood up.

"No argument there." Julian hugged his brother and sat in the rocking chair.

"How about a brew?"

"Sure." Julian petted Rebel's head. The dog licked his hand.

A minute later, Tom came back with two beers.

Julian grabbed one and they clinked bottles. Tom sat on the chair next to him. They both sipped, and there was a moment of silence.

"How's Julia doing?" Tom said.

"She's home." He'd tell him about her infidelity another time. "Now it's a matter of wait and see."

"Tell her I hope she feels better."

"I will." He had more beer. "You talk to Mom lately?"

"I called on her birthday." Tom's ring clinked his beer bottle. "Left a message. Never heard back."

"That was a while ago."

"Julian, she doesn't accept who I am." Tom picked up a ball and threw it. It landed somewhere in a bunch of trees, and Rebel raced after it. "You're the only one who does."

"You're special."

"Most people say weird." Tom took the ball from Rebel's

mouth and threw it farther than the last time. The dog waited for it to land before taking off after it. "It's good to see you."

"Same here."

"Now tell me what's up." Tom took a slug of beer, his Adam's apple bobbing.

"Tom, I'm just going to say this and then we can talk about it."

Tom squirmed in his seat. "Now you're making me nervous."

"Someone's threatened to kill Julia."

"What?" Tom shot to his feet. "Who? What the—"

"I wanted to tell you when you came to see me at the hospital." The rest of the story came pouring out. Tom sat back down and listened silently, intently.

"No freaking way," he said afterward. "You should've told me. I'm pissed *and* hurt. You can't leave me out of this."

"I'm sorry . . . I was trying not to involve you until I had some idea as to how you could help."

"When it's a threat against you, I'm already involved. Not knowing puts me at a disadvantage."

"You're right. I'm sorry."

"We don't have time for that now." Tom put down his beer. "So what have you done about this threat?"

"I tried to get Evelyn's help, but she stonewalled me. I went back to Sunrise to see if I could find a link between the Wrights and Cough, maybe someone who had a malpractice suit against Wright. I talked to Leah, a nurse who took care of me when I was a patient there."

"I remember her. She seemed nice."

"She acted like she hardly knew me."

Tom's brows furrowed. "That's odd."

"But then a man who worked in maintenance at the hospital, Melvin, overheard us. He approached me—said it was someone Wright *didn't* operate on, five years ago. Now I had something I knew you could help me with."

"You find out anything else?"

"Melvin was supposed to meet me in the lobby and give me more details, but Evelyn Wright showed up and told me Melvin was unavailable. Said I should leave and never come back."

"That's pretty hostile."

"I caught up with Melvin after work. He said he couldn't talk but that the answer was in Sunrise. The next day, Cough ambushed me in my car. He knew I'd been at the hospital asking questions and intensified his threat against Julia."

Tom nodded. "Let me do some digging. And we don't talk on the phone."

"Understood." Julian waited a beat. "You still have that rifle?"

"Of course, but let's hope it doesn't come to that." Tom was a marksman, having taught himself while working at a rifle range.

"I agree."

"First let's find out *who* we're up against." Tom picked up his beer. "Come by tomorrow—I should have something for you then."

———

The next day Julian was back on Tom's porch. Rebel was playing with a pup, the two dogs rolling around in a patch of dirt.

"Rebel is a bad influence on Buzz." Tom gazed at the two animals playing as he gently rocked his chair. "I couldn't find anything about Wright not operating on a patient, but the hospital's database only goes back three years."

"Melvin said it's in Sunrise." An idea was forming. "Wonder what condition the medical records are in."

"Too bad we just can't ask to see them."

"We can." Julian grinned.

"You got a plan?"

"I do." He had the steps in his head. "Someone has to ensure they're in order."

Now Tom was grinning. "You mean like auditors?"

"Exactly."

CHAPTER 20

"Mrs. Swanson is in charge of records." The heavyset female receptionist pointed to the far corner. "Take the service elevator to the basement and follow the signs to the administration offices."

Julian and Tom walked down a long corridor to an elevator. They wore suits and ties. Julian had on glasses and a fake mustache, and his hair was parted instead of combed straight back.

"That was easy," he said as they rode down.

"We haven't gotten to the hard part yet." Tom adjusted Julian's mustache.

"I know." He pushed his glasses farther up his nose. "Auditors don't usually get the friendliest receptions." He had firsthand experience with that.

"Where do you want to start?" Tom said.

Julian had given this some thought. "The death records."

"Fair enough."

The elevator opened. They headed right and walked single file until they arrived at a door with *Administration* on it.

A woman with glasses and short dark hair was seated behind a desk.

"Good morning," Tom said. "Are you Mrs. Swanson?"

"Yes."

"We're from the state. We're here to audit your records. It won't take long—no more than a couple of hours and we'll be out of your way."

Mrs. Swanson scowled. "I wasn't informed of this."

"We had a situation in another hospital." Julian put down his briefcase. "I'm not at liberty to discuss specific details, but it involved missing and incomplete records. Now the comptroller wants to make sure we don't have a similar problem in other locations."

"Needless to say," Tom whispered behind his knuckles, "it hit the fan."

"If you'd like to see some identification?" Julian reached his inside pocket. Tom had made convincing IDs for both of them.

"Please," she said. "After all, these are medical records."

"No problem." They handed their IDs to Mrs. Swanson. Julian watched her eyes move between them and their photos. Finally, she handed them back.

"What years do you want to see?"

"Our scope is the last ten," Julian said.

"We have the last seven here." Mrs. Swanson crossed her arms in front of her chest. "The rest are in an upstate warehouse."

"We'll start here and see how it goes." Julian nodded slowly, trying to look thoughtful. "We can increase the sample size to make up for the shorter period of time."

"I'll show you where they are." A set of keys jangled as she pulled them from her drawer and opened a door at the rear of the office. "This way."

Inside were rows of metal shelves filled with cardboard boxes.

"Where would you like to start?"

"The death records," Tom said.

"Follow me." Mrs. Swanson held her head high as she moved along. "I'm in charge of this department. Have been for the past twenty years."

"Certainly seems well-organized," Tom said. "This won't take long."

The place couldn't have been neater. The shelves were evenly spaced, and so were the boxes on them. The floors were clean, the air wasn't musty, and there was no dust as far as Julian could see.

Mrs. Swanson came to a halt.

"The death records, back to 2003." She pointed. "They're marked, in the last row." She glanced at each of them. "Anything else?"

"Looks like we got it from here."

"Yep." Tom smiled. "I mean 'yes.'"

"Good." Mrs. Swanson checked her watch. "I'll be here until three. I assume you'll be done by then?"

"We'll stop in and see you before we leave," Tom said.

"You don't plan on taking any documents or making copies, do you?" Mrs. Swanson planted her hands on her hips.

"No, ma'am." Tom showed her his palms. "As long as everything is in order, we'll be done and on our way"

"If there happen to be any discrepancies," Mrs. Swanson said, "I expect to see them *before* you report them. I can often explain the reason that necessitated the particular variance."

"We'll be sure to do that," Tom said.

"Good." She turned and left.

Julian rose up on his toes and looked around. There were at least a dozen rows of records.

"Do you think that might've been a little too easy?" Tom said once the sound of Mrs. Swanson's heels ceased.

"That or we're just good actors." Julian pulled down a box. Its printed label said "Death Records 2005." He and Tom crouched next to it. There were twelve green folders inside, one for each month of the year. He felt like he was invading someone's privacy—people whose lives had ended.

"Let's start with May." He slipped out the folder and opened it. It was stiffer than a manila one, as if in reverence to the significance of the documents inside. These were branches on a family tree, information a person might search for to learn about their predecessors. He flipped a page, making sure he didn't crease it. The paper was heavy and hard to separate. The documents were in alphabetical order. He had no idea what he was looking for.

Ackerman's certificate didn't refer to Dr. Wright or anything else that rang a bell. Neither did Bailey's. After *Dennis,*

Julian's eyes began to consistently land on the last names, so he moved through the file faster. If nothing popped the first time, he'd go through it again more slowly.

After twenty minutes or so, he came to Marcy Store.

He moved the file so that it was right under the fluorescent ceiling light. Marcy had died at twenty from a reaction to anesthesia. Her mother was named Beth. Her father was Neal Store.

The witness to the accident.

"This is it." He handed Tom the file. "The witness's daughter died in Sunrise."

"So Store might be Cough?" Tom said after he looked up from the document.

"And he's lying about what he saw." Sweat slicked Julian's skin. "Which means I'm guilty."

"I'm not convinced," Tom said. "Either way, we still don't know the details. That could put things in a different light. Let's keep looking."

"Let's cross-reference with Human Resources." Julian pulled himself up by holding on to the metal shelving. "I'll start from the top." He stepped lightly on the bottom shelf and retrieved a box labeled "Crenshaw R - Z." He put it on the floor and removed the lid. The files were by last name. "Here's a file for Alan Wright."

Tom stepped over a box and crouched beside him.

Julian flipped through a stack of memos. There was one about Wright's making a donation to the hospital on October 5, 2009.

"Wright gave fifty-thousand to Sunrise for undetermined purposes the Monday after the accident," he said. "It was made by Evelyn on her brother's behalf."

"That's a coincidence worth looking into," Tom said.

"There must be an accounting record for that transaction."

"Their general ledger system is online." Tom nodded. "I'll see what's there."

Julian continued reading, going back years. He stopped. At the back of the file, he found a memo:

> To: Files
> From: R. A. Crenshaw
> Subject: Mason and Store Surgeries
>
> On May 31, 2005, both Lyndon Mason and Marcy Store required brain surgery.
>
> Dr. Alan Wright operated on Lyndon Mason; Dr. William Line on Marcy Store. Ms. Store's surgery was less complex, but she did not survive her procedure.
>
> Because Mr. Mason was an alleged killer, it was called into question as to whether Dr. Wright should have operated on Marcy Store instead. Of the two surgeons, Dr. Wright had more experience.

The investigation revealed Ms. Store's death was the result of a severe allergic reaction to the anesthesia.

A committee looked into the matter and concluded that Drs. Wright and Line, as well as their respective surgical teams, followed best practices.

I contacted Mr. Store, informed him of our findings, and offered to meet with him to discuss it further. He declined my offer and said as far as he was concerned, the matter was closed.

Based on the events identified above, I'm considering this matter closed as well.

cc: Review committee

"Here are the details." Julian handed Tom the file.

"It fits." Tom looked up from the page. "I can't believe we actually found this."

"I'm guilty." Julian was numb. "If Wright had run the light, Cough wouldn't need to threaten me."

"That's one possibility," Tom said.

"Wright would've saved his daughter's life." Julian nodded slowly. "I bet that's what Store thinks. That gives him a motive for lying about what he saw."

"I'm reserving judgment until all the facts are in." Tom held a camera over the document. *Click*. "Now we got a copy." He flipped a page. Another click.

"What was that?"

"The members of the review committee. Just in case."

"I think we're done here." Julian closed his attaché. "We got what we came for."

CHAPTER 21

Julian and Tom were by the creek that ran behind Tom's cabin. Julian sat on a large boulder, balancing a pad on his knee. Tom, a few feet away, stood by the creek's shore. Sun bled through the leaves on the trees that lined the water. No other houses were in sight.

"Neal Store's wife, Beth, died of cancer last year." Tom threw something. It landed in the water with a plop. "His address is 29 Barker Avenue, Apartment 2A. He also owns a cabin in Kerhonkson. That's at 3216 Stratford Falls."

"Not so fast." Julian's hand had a cramp from writing so quickly. "I need to get all this down."

Tom never took notes. His teachers used to reprimand him for it, but he got good grades, so they let it go.

"Store was born in Sunrise on August 10, 1956. He weighed seven pounds, six ounces—just to round out your perspective."

Julian looked up. "You didn't just get this from the Internet?"

"It's all out there." Tom shrugged. "You just need to get in."

"It's impressive. I'm serious. The things you can do amaze me."

"Thanks." Tom bowed his head. "Too bad Mom doesn't see it that way."

"Sorry." He looked up at the sky. Birds flew in a single formation. "I can't help you with that."

"Just be my brother, Julian. That's all I ask."

"That I can do."

"Good." Tom threw another rock. It skidded along the top of the water and disappeared, sending out ripples. "Store is a licensed locksmith. He got a pistol permit when he started his business."

"You think the two are related?" Julian starred that note.

"That's what I figured." Tom boosted himself onto the boulder and peered over Julian's shoulder.

"Still, we need to be careful."

"No argument there."

"Does he have a degree?"

"In engineering." Tom's eyes moved up to the left. "Store would've had a 4.0 had it not been for a B in art his senior year."

"He sounds smart." Julian slapped the back of his neck, too late to stop a mosquito from sampling his blood. "College transcripts are hard to come by."

"I saw it and now it's here." Tom tapped the side of his

head. "He has dark hair and weighs one-sixty. Here's the problem: his DMV photo looks nothing like Cough, at least as you described him."

"Unless it's a disguise." Julian tapped his pen against the pad. "Let's get a closer look at him."

———

They sat in Tom's pickup on the south side of town watching Neal Store's apartment building. Tom had put a tracking device under the bumper of Store's decade-old sedan. The data went directly to Tom's cell and was backed up on his server.

"You don't see many of those," Tom said.

"What?"

"A fire escape." He pointed to the metal structures on the side of the building.

"They were big in the fifties." Julian watched a man and a woman cross the street in front of them, holding hands. They were young and looked happy.

"I feel like I'm missing something," Tom said.

"About Store?"

"No, my life." Tom had battled depression. At one time, he took medication for it. As far as Julian knew, he hadn't taken it in a while.

"You've got a lot of love, Tom. You just need the right person to give it to."

"Annie was supposed to be that one."

"You want to talk about it?" Julian turned in his seat so that he faced him.

"Not really. I mean I do, but I don't."

"You ever hear from her?"

"No." Tom rolled down the window and spit out it. "And I don't want to."

The pain was in Julian's gut.

Remember—

He's at the entrance to Julia's bedroom. He pushes the door. It opens. He smells her. A scent he loves.

"So when do I meet Julia?" Tom said.

"We're not exactly together right now." His stomach was still smarting, reliving his loss. "She cheated on me."

Tom looked stunned. "No."

"Says she's sorry." He shrugged. "Said it was an existential crisis."

"I had one of those. You start questioning life instead of living it."

"How'd you get over it?"

"Had my one and only one-night stand." Tom looked away from Julian's stare. "Wasn't seeing anyone at the time, still felt lousy about it the next day, but by the evening I was right as rain, knew I'd never do it again."

"How did that help?" Julian couldn't imagine Tom picking up a strange woman and bringing her home just for sex.

"I guess doing something out of character fries a circuit in your brain. Once you know who you're not, you rediscover who you are. Not saying I'd recommend it, but it did work for me."

"I want to forgive her," Julian said. "But I can't, not right now. Maybe never."

"You okay?" Tom said softly.

"I'm functioning."

"That's a start." Tom shook his head slowly. "When I found Annie in bed with Ray, of all people, I hurt for a while. I got over it, but I never want to go through that again."

Julian sucked in a breath and let it out in a rush. "I guess it's better to find out now rather than later."

"Even though it doesn't always feel that way."

"I hear you on that, brother."

Store's sedan appeared and turned right out of the complex. Julian pointed. "There he goes."

Tom started the truck, took off, and followed the silver vehicle at a safe distance. Julian snatched Tom's cell off the armrest and watched a blinking dot on an electronic map.

The dot went left.

Julian looked up and saw Store's sedan slide into a space between two cars in front of the Robbins Diner. Tom drove a little past and parked in a spot across the street. He'd always been good at finding parking spots when they were at a premium.

Store got out of his car and stretched. He had dark hair and was trim.

"Looks just like the pictures I've seen of him," Tom said.

"Doesn't look anything like Cough."

Store trotted up the steps and into the diner.

"Doesn't seem to have any trouble walking," Tom said.

"No, he doesn't." Julian zipped up his jacket. "Be right back."

He had on a baseball cap and a fake beard, and a pillow

was tucked inside his shirt. He looked chubby and waddled as he crossed the street with his head down and his hands in his pockets.

Inside, he found Store second in the take-out line. The diner was noisy, filled with an eclectic array of breakfast patrons with an occasional kid screaming. Julian hovered within earshot, surveying the dessert case as Store stepped up to the counter.

"Buttered bagel and coffee with cream, please," Store said.

The man behind the counter, whose name tag said *Pete*, wrote on a pad. "Anything else?"

"No, thank you."

"Be right back." Pete left.

Store eyed the selection of cakes, paying particular attention to the chocolate variety. Pete returned a minute later with a brown bag he handed to Store along with a slip of paper.

Store nodded, turned, and went over to the cashier. Two couples stepped in front of him as he got in line to pay. One of the women bumped into him.

Store coughed. A minute or two later he paid and walked out the front door.

Julian watched Store's sedan exit the parking lot from the diner's lobby. He had coughed, but it hadn't sounded right. Maybe he and Tom were wrong?

————

The next morning they were staked out again in front of Store's apartment building. Based on the data from the tracking device Tom had hidden under Store's vehicle, they knew he went out regularly at nine o'clock and would be gone for about an hour.

"Let's see if he kept that window open." He and Tom got out of the truck.

They walked a winding asphalt path, guided by metal railings in need of painting. A squirrel ran past them, its claws scratching the ground. There was a line of woods to the left, hiding a second road. An occasional honk of a horn or screech of a tire betrayed the nature scene. A four-story red-brick building with a rusting fire escape was now in front of them. Store lived in a corner unit, Apartment 2A.

"Look." He pointed to Store's window. It was partly open.

Tom gazed up, his hands on his hips. "I could climb this thing."

"I'll do it." Julian's insides quivered as he stared at the ladder he'd just committed to ascending

"There are other ways."

"Not as fast as this one." He recalled a summer they'd spent in the Hamptons when they were teenagers. Racing on the beach, swimming across the bay, lying on the dock after, nights spent stargazing. All good times. Then something changed between them. This wasn't how he'd have planned it, but he and Tom were finally getting back some of what they'd lost—a part of him he hadn't even realized he'd been missing.

"You ready?" Tom said.

"My phone is charged and on 'vibrate.'" Julian patted his cell, fastened to his hip.

"I'll call when I'm by the car." Tom was walking backward. "Don't go in until I do."

———

"All clear." Tom sounded out of breath. "Good luck."

"Thanks." He put his phone away, reached for the ladder—and heard barking.

An older woman with a white fluffy dog came toward him.

He ducked behind the building, his back against a chilly brick wall. His pulse raced as he peeked around the corner.

The dog was right below Store's window. It had a wiry white coat and round black eyes. It put its nose to the ground. The small creature went back and forth, circled, and squatted. It finished its business and returned to all fours.

The woman took out a tissue and a plastic bag from her pocketbook. She cleaned up after her pet as it watched her, wagging its tail. Finally she and the terrier walked away.

Julian waited until they were out of sight before going back to the ladder. He jumped, grabbed the bottom rung, and yanked it down as far as it would go. He executed a chin-up on the first rung and then exerted himself to wrap his fingers around the second. The iron bars dug deep into the meat of his palm as he made his way higher.

He continued up the ladder to the first floor. Luckily, the shades were drawn. He hurried up the metal staircase, his breathing becoming labored as he reached the second floor and came to a thriving spider plant. Beside it, a lounge chair had a coffee can attached to its arm by a copper wire.

The window was open a crack. Julian lifted it higher. He looked both ways one last time, then maneuvered his way in.

Inside, he faced a large blue recliner with a lamp next to it. On the other side of it was a table with a corded telephone and an ashtray with two butts in it. A wooden console television sat across from a blue couch covered in plastic.

He came to an oak dining room table with four place mats and a fake plant in the middle. A good-size cage of some sort sat in the corner. Except for the ashtray contents, the place was immaculate. The refrigerator hummed. Everything looked normal, but what had he expected—pictures of Wright and newspaper clippings plastered on the walls?

"Step up," an odd voice said. "Step up."

Julian spun on the ball of his foot and was confronted by a small green parrot with a blue head and a bar in each claw. He extended his index finger toward the bird, which immediately attacked the weapon invading its home. Julian jerked his hand back in the nick of time. The bird screeched and flapped its wings.

Julian continued on.

The kitchen counters were clear. The sink held a lone glass.

He went into the bedroom. The queen-size bed was made. A plug-in air freshener emitted a woody aroma. A lumber-jack shirt hung on a closet door, and a picture of a young girl was on the nightstand. She had blond hair and cradled a basketball. He picked up the frame. The girl in the picture was smiling. There were two block initials on the basketball: M.S. Marcy had died at twenty. So much more she could have done. Time stolen from her.

He parted the sliding mirror doors. A third of the closet held men's suits and slacks. The rest of the hanging clothes were dresses, skirts, and blouses. Shoes lined the closet floor—some men's, most women's, with an assortment of high heels, flats, and sandals. In a corner of the closet was a dark-haired wig with strands of gray.

He took a breath. This was it.

His cell rang. Tom.

"He's on his way back. Get out of there, Julian."

"It hasn't been an hour—"

"Now!"

"I'm at the window, okay?"

"Step up," the parrot said. "*Cough, cough.*"

Half out the window, Julian froze. But only for a second.

"Step up. *Cough, cough.*"

———

They drove back to Tom's cabin and stood together in front of the fireplace.

"The bird coughed." Julian shuddered.

"And the wig?"

"It was similar to Cough's hair." Julian recalled it propped up on its stand.

"Store's wife had cancer. It could have been hers—it

sounded like he kept all her things. And that's where you saw the wig, right? With her clothes?"

"Or hers and Marcy's clothes." Julian shook his head. "It's incriminating, but . . . something doesn't feel right."

"I agree." Tom picked up a bottle of tequila and poured some into Julian's glass.

He hadn't planned on a second, but as the distilled liquid worked its way through his system, the numbing sensation relaxed him. "Did you find out anything interesting on the Wrights?"

"Wright senior was an accomplished neurosurgeon." Tom slowly poured himself a shot, filled to the brim. "And Wright's wife, Evelyn, had bi-polar disorder."

"Both kids named after the parents?" Julian sipped some tequila.

"Yep. Wright junior failed his boards the first time. Passed at the top of his class the second. He did have a slew of parking tickets when he was doing some pro-bono work in the city, but he paid them all off. No other legal woes."

"What about his sister?"

"Evelyn junior has a bachelor's in pharmaceutical science. Never pursued it as a career, though."

"I could see her brewing concoctions." Julian shivered. "She gives me the willies."

"I'd like to meet her."

"Be careful what you wish for." He elbowed Tom. "What was in the agreement you were telling me about earlier?"

"When Wright's father died, he gave the kids five million and set up a trust fund. Each child needs to earn at least fifty thousand a year after the age of twenty-five to get their annual million-dollar payout."

"Not much of a problem for a brain surgeon."

"And Wright put his sister in charge of his foundation at the hospital. She makes a thousand a week."

"Fifty-two a year."

"They're probably set for a number of lifetimes."

"No other relatives?"

"Only Wright senior's wife. She has a sister who's currently in a mental institution."

"Both sisters with mental problems?"

"Yup, both on Evelyn's side—her mother and her aunt. Evelyn and Alan junior had different mothers. Alan's mother died in childbirth."

"We need to tell Slattery what we found out about Store," Julian said. "I'll be curious to see what he thinks."

"You trust him?" Tom said.

"I don't have a lot of options."

"We can figure it out together."

"I appreciate you wanting to protect me, but this way is faster and this needs to end quickly. It's best for everyone, myself included. I need your help and Slattery's—he's a professional, an ex-cop."

"Slattery doesn't care if you wind up in jail."

"Tom, someone died. If I'm responsible, that's my fate."

"Julian, I've seen these guys. They're nice and act like your buddy, but they're really looking for a way to cuff you."

"I think Slattery does the right thing no matter which way it turns out."

"Sounds like you *do* trust him."

"He's getting his chance."

CHAPTER 22

*J*ulian dialed Slattery's cell number.

"You remembered?" Slattery said after he picked up.

"Not yet. But I think the three of us should meet."

"Who's the third?"

"My brother, Tom. Is that a problem?"

"None at all," Slattery said. "The more the merrier." There was a pause. It sounded like he'd taken a hit on a cigar. "You have some information?"

"Yes. But it's also about us working together so we can get to the truth faster."

"You've come to the right place."

"Can we meet at my brother's tomorrow at two?"

"Give me the address."

———

Julian got to Tom's house the next morning and found him in front of his cabin chopping logs with an ax. He worked feverishly, each stroke splitting the log cleanly in two. He'd toss a completed piece into a pile and move on to the next. He put down his ax when he saw Julian.

"Looks like a storm is brewing," Tom said. "Could you help me get this wood in the shed?"

"Sure." He and Tom started tossing logs into the enclosure. Tom would chuck in a piece, and then Julian. After almost colliding once, they slowed down a bit. Julian couldn't recall the last time they'd worked together like this. When they finished, he wished they had more to do.

"I checked out the members of the committee that investigated Marcy's death." Tom closed the door on the woodshed and threaded the padlock through its latch. "It was comprised of a surgeon, an anesthesiologist, and the coroner, John McKenna."

"That seems to make sense." Julian saw a thick dark cloud in the distance, working its way toward them. "I'm assuming Wright is in the clear as far as Marcy goes."

"Yep." Tom started jogging. "Come on. It's gonna rain soon. Let's get some cover."

In no time, the two of them were in rocking chairs on the porch. Tom put his heels up on the railing.

"I was finally able to trace that donation Wright made to Sunrise shortly after the accident," he said. "The money went to Josh Industries. It's a sole proprietorship—a new consulting firm. The principal is John McKenna."

"The coroner from the committee?" Julian sprang from his chair and paced the porch. "Maybe he's doing some kind of outside work for them?"

"Maybe, but what kind of outside work would a coroner be doing?"

"If there *is* something nefarious going on, it could mean Marcy didn't die from the anesthesia."

"It's also possible the payment has nothing to do with Marcy." Tom crossed his arms over his chest. "However, the proximity to the accident at least raises the possibility it is connected." Tom shoved a toothpick into his mouth. "Need to get logical."

It started to rain, hard. Puddles deepened.

Julian leaned against the entrance, precipitation spraying his cheek. He checked his watch.

"Slattery should be here soon," he said.

"Before he gets here, let's take a peek at the coroner's report."

———

"Cheryl was drunk the night of the accident." Julian and Tom were seated on the couch in Tom's office. "Or as Evelyn told me, she was *inebriated.*"

"Not according to this report." Tom held up a document. "Cheryl had no alcohol in her system when she died."

"It could be a mistake." Julian doubted it was—how do you make a mistake like that? "I say we tell Slattery about this and see what he can come up with."

"Your call."

There was a chime. Tom went over to his computer—he had a motion camera by the entrance, and the feed showed on the monitor.

"Slattery just pulled into the driveway."

"I'll go greet him." Julian got up and headed toward the front door.

"Be right there." Tom called out. "Just gathering some documentation for the meeting."

———

Julian watched the investigator pull in next to his car. Slattery got out.

"Your brother ever think about getting that paved?" Slattery flung his thumb over his shoulder. The ground was muddy.

"He's thought about it." Julian grinned.

Tom came out onto the front porch.

"This better be worth it." Slattery held up his pant legs and gingerly waded through muck and mire. "If the GPS didn't know the address, I never would've found this place."

"Would you like something to drink?" Tom shook Slattery's hand.

"Ice water." Slattery leaned his head back. "Nice mountain."

"Tom owns it," Julian said.

"Your own personal precipice?" Slattery pushed up the brim on his fedora. "That's one for the bucket list."

"Let's go inside." Tom waved them in.

Julian sat directly across from Slattery at a round oak table. Tom emerged from the kitchen.

"Figured we could all use a clear head." Tom handed out ice water to everyone and then sat next to Julian.

"I spoke to a friend at the police station." Slattery sipped some water. "They had no arrest warrants, open cases, or complaints for anyone fitting Cough's description."

Julian looked at Tom. He nodded.

"Neal Store's daughter died at Sunrise during brain surgery." Julian gave Slattery a copy of the Crenshaw memo. "This gives you the details."

"You suspect Store is Cough?" Slattery said after he finished reading the document.

"That's our working hypothesis," Julian said.

"Though he'd have to have used a disguise," Tom said. "Which isn't out of the question."

"It was five years ago." Slattery seemed to be thinking something over. "Some say revenge is a dish best served cold."

"Store's wife passed away from cancer last year," Julian said. "Maybe that put him over the edge."

"Or it's a setup." Tom stared at him. "Julian, you look like you have an idea."

"Store's going to be a witness at the trial. Have Wright's attorney put him under pressure and see how he reacts."

"Like getting him to cough?" Slattery said.

"In a manner of speaking," Julian said.

"That might work." Slattery nodded. "Though I'll have to tell her about Cough."

"I understand," Julian said. "I'm good with that."

Tom frowned.

"I'll speak with Shelia and get her opinion," Slattery said. "Wright's attorney is a straight shooter."

"Do you know anything about Wright's health problem?" Tom had his elbows planted on the table.

"Not yet." Slattery bit his upper lip. "Evelyn and Dr. Wright haven't exactly been forthcoming on that topic. But the trial starts soon. We'll find out then."

"Wright's foundation donated fifty thousand to Sunrise on October 5, 2009." Julian handed Slattery a copy of the document from Crenshaw's files.

"You guys have been busy." Slattery read the memo and looked up. "It's interesting, but it doesn't change the color of the light."

"Tom was able to trace the accounting for that money and discovered it went to Josh Industries, a company with no prior sales. It's owned by John McKenna, the coroner."

"That definitely needs to be checked out." Slattery nodded. "I can take care of that."

"There's more." Tom handed Slattery a document. "We perused Cheryl Star's coroner's report, which doesn't mention her blood alcohol level being elevated even though she was supposedly drunk."

"Can I get a copy of this?" Slattery flipped through the pages. "I want to see if it jibes with mine."

"You can have that." Tom put his hands in his back pockets.

"I'll look into it." Slattery folded the report and slid it into his jacket. "I'd better catch John before he retires."

"The coroner's leaving?" Tom's tone rose.

"Put his papers in last week," Slattery said. "Heard he's moving to Costa Rica."

"That's interesting timing," Julian said.

"It is," Slattery said. "Enough to make you start thinking about things differently." He stood. "I'll call Wright's attorney and tell her about Store and Cough. She'll want to meet."

———

Shelia Black was thin, in her forties, wore black glasses, and had short dark hair.

"You want to help me prove Store *isn't* a credible witness?" Shelia was seated across from Julian. Slattery and Tom flanked him. They were in a conference room at the attorney's offices.

"I want you to make sure he isn't Cough." Julian had his palms flat on the table.

"If he is, it means you're almost certainly guilty." Shelia popped up from her seat and leaned on the top of her high-back chair.

"Someone's life is at stake here," he said. "That trumps everything else."

"My brother is trying to do the right thing," Tom said. "Can't you see that?"

"Yes." Shelia was staring at Julian. "My gut says I should trust you, and I do."

"Do you think the DA is aware of what happened to Store's daughter?" He knew Shelia already had copies of all pertinent documentation regarding the incident.

"Yes, and if Hawkins is as good as I think he is, he'll ask Store about it before I cross-examine him."

———

"Is there anything I can do?" Julian said. He and Slattery were on the phone. The trial would begin the next day.

"Just show up. Your perspective is paramount."

"Tom and I will be there."

"Good. Store is the first witness. Don't be late."

———

The night before the trial, Julian was studying the bedroom ceiling at 2 a.m., thinking about Julia.

She'd left a message. He hadn't gotten it until late—he'd call her in the morning. Sometimes their conversations flowed as if nothing were wrong. Other times, there were long pauses.

Now he could feel the sensation of her head on his chest. He missed her. He still hadn't forgiven her, but at least the detective work with Tom and Slattery was a distraction from the worst hurt his heart had ever known.

CHAPTER 23

Julian stood in front of a courthouse that took up an entire city block. Fluted columns flanked two double doors at the entrance. Honking cars filled the streets.

A black limousine pulled up to the curb. Wright got out. His sister, close behind, slid her arm through his.

Wright went up the courthouse steps sandwiched between his sister and his attorney. Four reporters swarmed him. Three were male and older. One was a young woman with big dark eyes and short blond hair.

Evelyn put her arm around her brother. She and Shelia shooed the reporters away and continued up to the landing and into the building.

Julian made his way up the courthouse steps.

"Mr. Barncs," the female reporter said. A cameraman was behind her. "Have you had any further recollections of the accident?"

"I'm sorry," he said.

"You have nothing to say?" She squished her eyebrows together.

"I'm required to be at these proceedings and they're about to begin." He went past her, entered the building, waited in line to get through a metal detector, and was directed to the second floor.

When he stepped off the elevator, he saw Wright, Evelyn, and Shelia approaching the courtroom.

Julian's eyes met Evelyn's for a beat. Then she went inside. He shivered.

The digital clock above the threshold read 9:30. He sat three rows behind the prosecution.

The bailiff stood. "All rise for Judge Ronald Markham."

The judge walked in with flowing robes. Sixties, big, with bushy white hair and hazel eyes set deep in their sockets. He sat at the bench and banged his gavel. The people in the packed courtroom came to order.

"Defendant, please rise," the judge said.

Wright did as he was asked.

"Bailiff, please read the charges," the judge said.

"In the case of The People vs. Alan Wright, the charge is vehicular manslaughter in the second degree."

"Mr. Wright, how do you plead?" the judge said.

"Not guilty, Your Honor."

"The defendant may sit." Markham faced the twelve jurors split evenly between men and women. They all appeared attentive, except for a woman in the back row who fidgeted with a big black pocketbook. When she finally finished, the judge cleared his throat. "Mr. Hawkins, please proceed with your opening argument."

"Thank you, Your Honor." Hawkins buttoned his suit jacket as he sauntered toward the jury. "Ladies and gentlemen, this is a case about responsibility, and we're going to prove that Alan Wright acted *irresponsibly,* and that cost Cheryl Star her life." His gaze went toward the Stars, seated next to their attorney, who had on the same light-colored suit he'd worn for deposition. Trisha leaned on her husband with a balled tissue in her hand.

"Cheryl wasn't just a dedicated nurse," Hawkins said. "She was a daughter, a sister, and an aunt. One day she planned to be a wife and mother. Now she's gone." He walked the length of the jury box, his fingers lightly grazing its banister. "How would you feel if you lost a loved one because of someone else's irresponsibility? Would you accept it and move on?" A juror with a full beard and a red shirt shook his head. "I didn't think so. You'd want what any rational human would want. You'd want justice." Red shirt nodded. So did Hawkins. "You twelve can give the Stars that justice." He faced the judge. "Nothing further, Your Honor."

"Ms. Black," the judge extended a hand, "your turn."

"Thank you, Your Honor." Shelia approached the dozen people who would decide her client's fate. "The prosecution talks about responsibility. Yet they *irresponsibly* omit a crucial fact: Alan Wright didn't run a red light. He didn't cause the accident and therefore is *not* responsible for Cheryl Star's death." She was next to the red-shirted juror. "We'll present evidence that contradicts the witness's account of what happened." Her gaze went from Julian back to the jurors. "Ladies and gentlemen, the wrong person is on trial here. Dr. Alan Wright is another victim in this crime, and as far as making restitution for all parties involved goes, that's not a marker of guilt but rather one of character. My client is innocent of any wrongdoing whatsoever. You're about to discover that. Thank you. Nothing further, Your Honor." The attorney headed to her seat.

Wright stared straight ahead, jaw tight.

Julian imagined himself in Wright's position: the whole world here to scrutinize him, the embarrassment he'd feel knowing he was guilty, and no recourse but to let a group of strangers judge and sentence him. He shuddered.

"Mr. Hawkins," Judge Markham said, "please proceed."

Julian heard a door open and turned around. Tom was seating himself in the back row. He'd said he'd be a little late. They exchanged a nod. Slattery, next to him, appeared to be reading something in his lap.

"The prosecution calls Neal Store to the stand," Hawkins said.

A man in his forties rose. He had gold horn-rimmed glasses and dark hair and wore a black suit, a tie, and a white shirt. His complexion was light and his nose was covered in thread-thin veins. After he was sworn in and seated in the witness chair, the district attorney approached him.

"Mr. Store, please tell us *exactly* what you saw on the night in question," Hawkins said.

"I was walking along Brewster. It was a clear evening. The stoplight was to my right. It was red. Dr. Wright's car approached it without slowing. It wasn't speeding—it just kept going as if the light was green. I remember thinking, *That car isn't going to stop.*" He paused. "And it didn't. It broadsided the other vehicle. There was a loud crash and a horn went off. I immediately called 911, then I ran to the scene of the collision . . . I had to wait for a cab to pass before I could cross the street. The police and the ambulance arrived within minutes. The paramedics attended to the passengers, and Officer James stopped the horn from blowing. I gave a statement to him and left."

"Were there any other civilians on the scene?" Hawkins said.

"Ms. Wright came not long after." Store looked toward where Evelyn sat. "And then Ms. Dee, the nurse, a few minutes later."

"Did anything peculiar happen that night? Any event that sticks out in your mind as strange?"

"No. It was all very straightforward. I never imagined I'd be a witness at a trial."

Hawkins was halfway to his table when he stopped and spun around.

"Mr. Store, have you or your family ever been a patient at Sunrise Hospital?" he said.

"I was born there." Store's gaze appeared to be unfocused. "And my daughter was treated there."

"What was the result of her stay?" Hawkins approached the witness.

"She died during a brain surgery," he said softly.

"Did Dr. Wright perform the operation?"

"No." Store covered his mouth. "He was supposed to."

"What happened?"

"He operated on someone else because theirs was a more complicated procedure."

"How did you feel about that?"

"I questioned it, since the surgeon who operated on Marcy was far less experienced than Dr. Wright. The hospital's investigation concluded she died from an allergic reaction to the anesthesia and it wouldn't have made a difference who performed the surgery."

"And what was your reaction?" Hawkins said.

"I accepted their explanation."

"How long ago was this?"

"Five years."

"And you've had no contact with the hospital since?"

"That's correct."

"Thank you, Mr. Store, for your testimony," Hawkins said. "No further questions, Your Honor."

"Ms. Black," Markham said, "please proceed with your questioning."

Shelia rose. "Mr. Store, do you have any doubts about what you saw?" She was in front of him, spinning her glasses.

"None whatsoever."

"Really." She donned her spectacles. "No time since this all happened where you wondered if you really *hadn't* seen what you thought you had?"

"Can't recall one." He shifted in his seat.

"You weren't driving, so you had no need to pay attention to what was happening." Her gaze went toward Wright. "As opposed to Dr. Wright, a brain surgeon, who had every reason to be aware of his surroundings." She returned her attention to Store. "Who would you put your money on?"

"Objection." Hawkins was seated. "The witness has already answered the question twice."

"Let's continue, Ms. Black," Markham said, "but use this time productively."

"Yes, Your Honor." She turned toward the witness. "There were two events." She held up the corresponding number of digits. "The color of the light *and* the crash itself." She peered at the witness. "You saw both simultaneously?"

"I was far enough away where I had that perspective." Store closed his eyes. "I've played it in my mind dozens of times. The red light is the first thing I see. From the corner of my eye, the black Porsche approaches. The front of the other car was already in the intersection. The collision is a solid hit. I can still hear the glass breaking." He shook his head slowly. "And that incessant horn."

A shrill sob pierced the courtroom.

Everyone's eyes were on Trisha Star. Her husband had an arm around her.

"Mrs. Star," the judge said, "I realize this must be very difficult for you."

"Thank you, Your Honor." Trisha dabbed her eyes with her tissue and sat up straight. "But I'm better now."

"Ms. Black," Markham said, "please resume your cross-examination."

"Mr. Store, did you have a drink on the night in question?" She leaned an elbow on the wooden wall that surrounded the witness.

"Yes." He cleared his throat. "I went to Pat's. It's right down the block from Brewster."

"What did you have there?"

"A vodka martini."

"Those are pretty powerful." She raised her chin as if she were impressed.

"That's why I only had one."

Shelia gazed at Julian. He shrugged, barely.

"Mr. Store," she said, "how long after you finished your *martini* did you leave Pat's?"

"Five minutes. No more than ten. I wanted to get home to watch the evening news."

"Were you driving?"

"No. I live in the area."

"You probably didn't want to be behind the wheel after one of those martinis?" Shelia chuckled.

"I didn't break any laws, Ms. Black."

"How much do you weigh, Mr. Store? One seventy?"

"That's about right."

"How many ounces of alcohol are in one of those martinis?"

"Three shots," he said.

"Three ounces." Shelia approached the jury. "Mr. Store would not have had enough time to metabolize enough alcohol to be under the legal driving limit when he left Pat's and witnessed the accident."

"I wasn't driving, Ms. Black. I was walking."

"Your judgment was impaired." She frowned. "You've got to consider that a possibility."

"Objection." Hawkins rose. "The defense attorney's assertion is unfounded. The officer at the scene stated that the witness was coherent when he gave his account of the events and that there was nothing suspicious about him at all."

"Withdrawn." She peered at Store. "Mr. Store, you can state unequivocally that you have no animosity toward Dr. Wright as a result of Marcy's death?"

"None whatsoever."

"Even though Dr. Wright operated on a murderer instead of her?"

Cough. Store covered his mouth.

Julian's heart raced. Store wasn't Cough. The sound, the mannerisms—it was all off.

"Your Honor." Hawkins stood. "She's provoking the witness. What's going on here?"

"Ms. Black?" the judge said. "Can you explain?"

"Your Honor, I need a twenty-minute recess."

"I'll assume it's urgent and you won't make this a habit?" Markham scowled.

"It is and I won't."

The judge banged the gavel. "Court recessed until then."

———

"I don't think it's him," Julian said. He, Tom, Slattery, and Shelia were in a meeting room at the courthouse.

Shelia patted her midsection. "My gut reaction is he's not the one making the threats, *but* his account of the accident is inaccurate." She looked at her wristwatch. "I've got to get back to the courtroom. Slattery, do you need anything else from me?"

"No. We've got it from here." Slattery stood. "Thank you, Shelia. We'll let you know if we come up with something."

"Call me any time. I won't be sleeping for a while." She was already by the entrance. "Now I need to prepare for the next witness." She departed, closing the door behind her.

There was a moment of silence. Julian was about to get up. Slattery put his hand on his shoulder. Julian sat back down.

"Cheryl's blood alcohol level *was* incorrect on the coroner's report." Slattery's gaze rested on each of them momentarily. "Evelyn and the coroner, John McKenna, were an item at one time."

"We didn't know that," Tom said.

"Now you do." Slattery grabbed his own lapels. "Let's go over the facts we have."

"Wright's foundation sent money to McKenna," Julian said.

"There was a mistake on the autopsy report, which was made by McKenna," Tom said. "McKenna and Evelyn were lovers. And now he's retiring?" Tom sniffed. "Something doesn't smell right."

"I hear you, but why would they pay McKenna to keep Cheryl's alcohol level off the autopsy report?" Slattery rubbed his chin. "Doesn't make sense."

"The error on the report could've just been a mistake," Julian said. "The payment could be for something else. Maybe it's related to Cough?"

"Maybe he's Cough?" Tom said.

"Wait a minute." Slattery showed them his meaty palm. "I agree Store isn't Cough, but other than that, we're just speculating. I've known John for a while. I don't see him wearing a wig and prancing around the hospital in the middle of the night threatening someone. I'm not saying he wouldn't be above a little payola if the money was right, but nothing physical." He shook his head. "He's just not that kind of guy. I could be wrong, but I think there are better places to look." He adjusted his tie. "What we could use is a lead."

"Like my remembering the accident," Julian said

"I bet some of the answers are at Sunrise," Tom said.

"I agree." Slattery rose. "That's why I'm paying the hospital a visit. I bet there's a lead or two there." He waved them on. "Come on, the trial is about to resume."

CHAPTER 24

*B*ack in the courtroom, Julian returned to his seat. Tom moved up to sit beside Julian, and Slattery was positioned behind the defense.

"The prosecution calls Angela Dee," Hawkins said once the proceedings resumed.

The woman who came to her feet was in her thirties and wore heels and a red pantsuit. Her short dark hair complemented her round, pretty face.

"Ms. Dee," Hawkins said after the bailiff stepped away from the witness, "do you work with the defendant?"

"Yes, I'm an operating room nurse and assist Dr. Wright on most of his surgeries." Her gaze drifted toward Wright, who wouldn't look at her. "We've worked together for three years."

"Did you know Cheryl Star?"

"She was a co-worker and a friend."

"When did you last see Cheryl?"

"On the night of October 2, 2009. There was a party for a nurse who was leaving. Cheryl had had too much to drink and was asleep in the front passenger seat of Dr. Wright's car. He was taking her home. I buckled her in." Angela produced a handkerchief. "I can still hear the click when the latch locked into place."

"Did Cheryl like to imbibe?"

"Not really. In fact, that was the strange part—Cheryl had told me she thought she might be pregnant."

Murmurs in the courtroom.

"She hadn't taken a test yet," Angela said, "so it wasn't definite. She said she just wouldn't drink, as a precaution."

"Let the record show," Hawkins said, "that according to a statement from the coroner, Ms. Star was *not* pregnant at the time of her death."

"When I saw her drunk," Angela said, "I figured she'd been mistaken on the pregnancy and got a little carried away over the fact that she'd found out Alan—I mean Dr. Wright—had been shopping for engagement rings."

"And she assumed the ring was for her?"

"Yes. They'd been together for over a year."

"So, Ms. Dee, Cheryl Star was so inebriated that she had no say in how she was getting home that night?"

"That's . . . correct."

"And on the evening of that same day, Ms. Dee, did you assist the defendant in a surgery?"

"Yes."

"How long did that procedure take?" Hawkins pulled up a pant leg and planted his shoe on the platform that surrounded the witness stand.

"We were going on four hours." She rubbed the arms of her chair.

"Is that long?"

"Not really. We've gone twelve."

"And was the operation successful?"

"No. Dr. Wright didn't remove the tumor."

"Why?"

"He said he wanted more time to study it."

"Does that happen often?" Hawkins said.

"Not with Dr. Wright, at least not until recently."

"What changed?"

"Lately, Dr. Wright has been having . . . difficulties."

"What kind of difficulties?"

"For one thing, he doesn't seem to have the endurance he once had."

"Could you give us an example?" Hawkins was next to the foreman of the jury, a young woman in her twenties. Red shirt was beside her, stroking his beard.

"He dozed."

Wright gave a start.

"It wasn't long, but he was definitely not conscious for a period of time during an operation. It was scary." Angela's chest rose as her gaze went toward the defense table. "Alan, I'm sorry, but I can't lie." She turned toward Markham. "Something is wrong with Dr. Wright."

"Ms. Dee." The judge pointed the gavel at her. "Stick to answering questions. No extemporizing, please. The prosecution may continue."

"Ms. Dee." Hawkins faced the jury. "Had you spoken to the defendant about his dozing?"

"Yes."

"When?"

"On . . . the night Cheryl died."

"What did he say?"

"He said . . . he was aware of the problem and was looking into it."

The court reporter's fingers moved rapidly over the keys. He was the same young man from the deposition.

"Ms. Dee," Hawkins said, "on the night of the accident, you told the doctor you would call a cab to take him and Cheryl home?"

"I did."

Voices from the courtroom. Markham raised his gavel and appeared to search for the offenders. Soon there was silence.

"What was the defendant's reply?" Hawkins said.

"He said he'd have some coffee and he'd be fine." She pinched her temples. "I should've done more. If I had, this wouldn't have happened."

"Ms. Dee, I'm sorry for any trauma this might have caused you."

"I appreciate your saying that, Mr. Hawkins, but I still can't help feeling I let Cheryl down."

"Your Honor, I reserve the right to recall Ms. Dee at a later time, but as of now, I have no further questions for her."

"Ms. Black, your witness," the judge said.

Shelia strode toward the stand.

"Ms. Dee, have you and Dr. Wright ever gone out socially?"

"We dated, if that's what you're referring to." She sat up straight. "But that was before I came to Sunrise."

"How did it end between you and the doctor?"

"Dr. Wright broke it off."

"Did he hurt you?" Shelia said.

"Objection, Your Honor," Hawkins said. "What's the relevance here?"

"My question goes to credibility, Your Honor."

Markham nodded. "Overruled, but please make your point, Ms. Black."

"Ms. Dee, is it true that you have been the most vocal about Dr. Wright's perceived problems?"

"That's because I work so closely with him."

"So it has nothing to do with his breaking your heart?"

"Objection," Hawkins said. "This line of questioning is inappropriate."

"Your Honor," Shelia said, "I have specific evidence to present regarding Ms. Dee's romantic past which I think is relevant to this case."

"Overruled," Markham said. "Ms. Black, please use the latitude I'm giving you judiciously."

"Ms. Dee, was a restraining order taken out against you in 2002?" Shelia held up a document for all to see.

"Yes." Angela hunched her shoulders.

"It was from a doctor at Weeks Memorial Hospital, where you worked at the time?"

Angela nodded.

"And it was because you refused to end your romantic relationship with him and had gone as far as making physical threats against him?"

"There's more to it than that—"

"No further questions, Your Honor." Shelia went back to her table.

The bailiff handed the judge a sheet of paper. Markham read it and pursed his lips.

"Let's adjourn here for the day," the judge said. "Court resumes Monday at nine thirty."

———

Julian was driving home from the courthouse. He had a headache—a bad one. Was this how Julia felt when she got one of hers?

His cell phone rang.

"Julian," Ruth said. "I could sure use your help."

"What's wrong?"

"It's Julia." Her voice was taut. "She's not well. More headaches."

"I didn't know. I was at the trial."

"She keeps mentioning you. Could you come over?"

"I'm on my way." He put on his blinker and changed lanes.

"Thank you so much. I'll leave the front door unlocked." She hung up.

Julian clutched the wheel tighter, kept within the speed limit, and headed toward Ruth's.

CHAPTER 25

Julian brought his car to a halt and bolted out of it.

"Hello?" His voice echoed toward the balusters on the second landing.

Silence.

"Hello," he said again, louder this time.

"We're up here," Ruth said.

He bounded up the stairs. At the top step, he heard retching. He ran toward the bedroom and found Ruth sitting in the rocking chair.

"She woke up with a pain in her head." Ruth had circles under her eyes. She nodded toward the bathroom. "Then she got nauseous. That was two hours ago. She's been in there ever since."

"You haven't checked on her?" Julian was about to when Ruth clutched his arm.

"Julian, I go in there every five minutes."

"I'm sorry, of course you do. I'm just—"

Julia appeared in the doorway. She was pale, eyes puffed, her hair tangled. She leaned against the jamb and then slowly slid to the floor in a fetal position.

He knelt by her.

"My head . . . It hurts." Julia had her cheek pressed against her clasped hands. "I can't take this anymore."

"Is it the same pain?"

"I'm not sure." Her face was contorted.

He tried to help her to her feet.

"No. Let me stay here. I . . . I can't move."

He picked her up anyway, carried her to the bed, and gently lowered her onto the mattress. She curled back up. Ruth wiped her face and arms with a washcloth and covered her with a blanket.

"I'm calling the doctor." He took out his cell, half-expecting Julia to tell him to wait. She didn't, and he wouldn't have stopped dialing no matter what she said.

The phone rang. Once, twice, three times. He felt his blood pressure surge and took a breath. Fourth ring, fifth, sixth ring—

"Doctor's answering service," a woman said. "Whom would you like to contact?"

"Dr. Rig. It's an emergency."

"I'll get him the message right away, sir. May I have your number?"

He gave it to her along with the pertinent details.

"Sir, please keep your line open." She hung up.

He'd give Rig ten minutes and then he'd call an ambulance.

Two minutes later his phone rang.

"Get her to emergency as soon as possible," Rig said after Julian described the symptoms. "I'm with another patient, but I'll be there after I finish up with them."

"What did the doctor say?" Ruth asked the minute Julian hung up.

"We need an ambulance." His mind was going in a million directions.

"Call 911," Ruth said.

He pressed 9, 1—

"No." Julia furrowed her brow. "Can you take me?"

"If you go in an ambulance, you'll be admitted to the emergency room right away." He took in a deep breath and let it out slowly, doing his best to stay calm.

"All that noise . . . It'll just make me worse." Julia propped herself up. "Mom, please help me get dressed."

He was about to speak.

"Please," Julia said, "let me do it this way."

Ruth raised her eyebrows.

"Okay," he said. "I'll be outside waiting."

———

They were in an area cordoned off by a curtain, Julia lying on a gurney. Ruth was sitting next to her, holding her hand. Julia's eyes were half-closed. She'd been given painkillers after being admitted.

The curtain parted and a nurse in her forties came in. She had a thick body and a stern look on her attractive face. *Rhonda* was on her name tag. Ruth released Julia's hand.

"The room ready?" Julian said.

"She might have to stay here tonight." Rhonda stepped past him and over to Julia. "You're lucky you're still not in the waiting room."

Julian bit his tongue. Had they gone by ambulance, she would have been admitted hours ago.

"I'm going to get some coffee." He stood and moved toward the exit. "Anyone need anything?"

"A hospital room." Julia gave him a weak smile.

"I could use a cup of coffee, too." Ruth held her lower back with both hands.

"You got it," he said.

"The cafeteria closes at nine." Rhonda wrapped a blood pressure cuff around Julia's bicep.

"I love you," Julia said just before a thermometer was stuck in her mouth.

He blew her a kiss and then slipped between the curtain.

———

Julian went past the waiting area for the emergency room. Two sliding glass doors parted. Outside, no one was in sight. He took in fresh air and then started walking. He was vaguely familiar with the area, but to ensure he didn't get lost, he went straight.

He passed single-family homes. Trees covered most of the sidewalks. His pulse climbed as he went uphill.

Rampant chirping. The sound got louder with each step. He passed underneath a willow filled with birds and sped up. Once it was behind him, he brushed off his shoulders and checked for droppings. Fortunately, there were none.

His legs found a steady pace. He hadn't planned on going far, but the movement was doing him good. He came to a corner. He was unsure how many he'd passed, but all he had to do was turn around.

He went three more blocks.

Suddenly, he pictured Julia convulsing on a gurney. He had to get back.

He spun around and sped up, almost jogging, then just short of running. If something had gone wrong and he wasn't around, they'd call his cell. He checked it, still in stride, and discovered it had been off since he first entered the hospital. He turned it on, frustrated he hadn't done it sooner. He perspired as the phone booted up. Would there be a message?

The phone beeped. Someone had called him. His heart pounded as he checked his recent calls. He sighed with relief when it turned out it had been Tom. He dialed Tom's number.

"What time is good to meet?" Julian said after they exchanged greetings.

"Let's see. I have a job interview at ten and another at two."

"You do?"

Tom laughed. "Kidding . . . I'll be home all day."

"You still looking?"

"I send out résumés, but I've yet to go on an interview. Right now I'm having a good time being your brother. Can we leave it at that?"

"Sure." Julian checked the time. "I told them I was going for coffee. I'd better go."

"Call me if you need anything."

"Thanks, Tom. I'll be there at ten. I love you, little brother, you know that?"

"It's mutual. See you tomorrow. Me and Rebel will be waiting for you." A click.

———

Julian raced back into the hospital and down a long corridor, following signs to the cafeteria. When he got there, it was closed, the entrance padlocked.

He jogged to the elevator and looked up at the number display—three, two, one, and B. A bell chimed and the doors drew back. He stepped inside and pressed the button for the first floor. The doors didn't close. He counted to ten—still no movement. He pressed the first-floor button again. Nothing. He bolted out of the cab, headed back to the stairwell, and ran up to the first floor. There he followed red signs to the emergency room.

He turned a corner and almost ran into Ruth.

"Where did you go?" she said.

"I was outside." He dug his hands into his pockets. "I must have lost track of time."

"That's not like you." She had Julia's eyes. "Where's my coffee?" And her spunk.

"The cafeteria was closed." His cheeks felt warm. "Sorry."

"Don't worry about it." Ruth patted his back. "We're all under a lot of pressure."

He was about to head to Julia when Ruth looped her arm through his and led him in the opposite direction.

"She's already asleep," Ruth said.

"What about the doctor?" Julian felt disoriented. "Did he come?"

"Right after you left."

"What did he say?" He leaned against a wall.

"He wants to talk to us tomorrow morning. I know it would mean a lot to Julia if you were there."

"I will be."

———

"The pain was a side effect of the medication I prescribed." Dr. Rig sat behind his desk. Julian and Ruth were seated in front of it. Julia was in a wheelchair next to them. "I've taken you off it, Julia. You should be getting relief shortly."

"I do feel better," she said.

"That's good news." Ruth leaned forward in her seat.

"The problem is the follow-up scans." Rig cleared his

throat. "The tumor might be growing. It's still a little too soon to judge—we're going to monitor it. It shouldn't stop you from resuming normal activities after you leave the hospital."

"Please tell me the truth, Doctor." Julia held the arms of her chair. "What's your best guess if the tumor grows?"

Rig folded his hands on the desk.

"*If* it does, and we don't know for sure that it will . . . I don't think you have more than a year."

CHAPTER 26

Julian was back at court, his mind still reeling from Julia's diagnosis.

Wright sat at the defense table, fingers folded in front of him. Those hands had saved lives. If he knew for certain Wright could cure Julia, all Julian would have to do was say that he remembered, that the accident was his fault. He'd jump to his feet and take the blame right now.

Judge Markham entered the courtroom and assumed his position on the bench.

"Mr. Hawkins, you may proceed with your case," he said.

"The prosecution calls Dr. Scott Andrews to the stand."

A man in his early forties approached the front of the courtroom. He had a short beard and wore a pinstripe suit. His initials were on his cuffs, a gold stickpin in his tie, and his loafers shimmered.

"Dr. Andrews, what is your area of expertise?" Hawkins said after the witness was sworn in.

"I am a board-certified neurologist who has practiced medicine in this area for the past twenty years."

"And do you testify at cases for a fee?"

"This is the first time." Andrews uncrossed his arms.

"You were hired by the people to assess Alan Wright's recent performance as a doctor in general and a surgeon in particular, is that correct?"

"Yes."

Shelia had a thick pen wedged between her fingers as she took copious notes.

"Please describe your fact-finding process," Hawkins said.

"I examined records, questioned hospital staff, and performed research," Andrews said. "There was a definite change in Dr. Wright."

"Can you be more specific?"

"He's had a lack of stamina. Ms. Dee's testimony as to his dozing supports that, and he's not been as decisive as he was in the past."

"Please describe an instance of his indecisiveness for the jury." Hawkins turned toward the jurors.

"During an operation, an artery erupted. It needed to be cauterized immediately or the patient would exsanguinate."

Hawkins looked at the witness quizzically.

"Bleed to death," Andrews said.

"Got it. Go on."

"Dr. Wright hesitated, as if confused. Bear in mind, this

would be a relatively routine problem for a neurosurgeon of his caliber. The physician's assistant had to step in and take over until Dr. Wright recovered. The incident was documented in the operating-room log."

Wright bowed his head.

"It's all in my report," Andrews said.

Hawkins held up a spiral-bound binder. "I would like the court to enter this as Medical Exhibit A," he said.

"Bailiff, please make sure copies are distributed to each member of the jury," Markham said.

"Dr. Andrews," Hawkins said, "did you identify any other changes in Dr. Wright during your investigation?"

"Yes, in his motor skills, as evidenced by his handwriting."

"Are you a handwriting expert?" Hawkins had his hands on his hips, suit coat pushed back, exposing his thin waist. He had a runner's body.

"I minored in graphology," Andrews said.

The bailiff brought an easel out and placed it so it faced the jury.

The doctor went over to the two enlarged Alan Wright signatures on display. The first was dated April 2005, the second August 2009.

"Now, there's a lot of information I can give you relative to someone's handwriting," Andrews said. "But for the purposes of this explanation, I'm going to focus on the basics." He put the tip of the pointer on the first signature. "Notice that the lines in this earlier example are straight. The loops are smooth and well-rounded. In the later example, the loops are uneven and the lines are jagged." He moved the pointer between the two signatures. "The variances indicate a loss of motor skills which *is* consistent with the other input I've received as a result of my investigation."

"Thank you, Dr. Andrews. That was enlightening." Hawkins took the pointer from the doctor and handed it to the bailiff.

Andrews returned to the witness stand.

"Doctor Andrews, could you tell us about the defendant's drug test at the time of the accident?" Hawkins raised his brow.

"It revealed he was on medication used to treat tremors."

"And, Doctor, based on all of your research, have you reached a conclusion?" Hawkins said.

"Objection, Your Honor." Shelia rose. "The witness has not physically examined Dr. Wright. We can't allow him to make a diagnosis based only on second-hand input."

"The witness is an expert, and this is his testimony based on his investigation." Markham brought his big bushy eyebrows together. "Overruled. Dr. Andrews, please answer the question."

"I would say . . ." Andrews straightened his cuffs. "It's a good possibility Dr. Wright is suffering from Lewy body dementia, or LBD."

A burst of chatter morphed into silence.

"What is that?" Hawkins said.

"A form of dementia whereby abnormal structures called Lewy bodies develop in regions of the brain that affect thinking and motor skills."

"Isn't the defendant too young to have dementia?"

"This particular disease can come at a younger age. The markers I've identified are clearly cognitive in nature, which is consistent with the symptoms of LBD."

"Please explain *cognitive.*"

"Ability to reason. His indecisiveness in the operating room would be an example of that."

"And is it possible, Dr. Andrews, that someone with Lewy body dementia could see a red light and think it's green?"

"It would depend on the circumstances, but yes, hallucinations can accompany the malady."

"And might that not be more likely at night?"

"From fatigue . . . Yes, could be."

Two jury members seated in the first row nodded. Shelia sat back in her seat and shook her head. Wright continued staring at the space in front of him. Burl sighed. The Stars held each other.

"Dr. Andrews, have you had patients with Lewy body dementia?" Hawkins said.

"Yes, a fair number."

"And Dr. Wright must have such patients as well?"

"I would say so."

"So he would have recognized these symptoms?"

"That's likely, yes."

Hawkins paused. "Doctor, what would happen if Dr. Wright decreased his caseload?"

"I believe his symptoms would be much less problematic."

"But he didn't."

"My findings are he did *not* take on fewer patients. In fact, he was taking on more."

"As if he were trying to treat as many as he could before—"

"Objection," Shelia said. Before she could say on what grounds, Hawkins said he had no further questions and returned to the prosecution's table.

"Ms. Black." The judge held his hand out toward the witness.

"Doctor, the anti-tremor medication you referred to . . . That's used to treat other conditions besides LBD, isn't it?"

"It could be."

"In fact, Dr. Wright has been treated for sciatica, and this very same anti-tremor medication has been proven effective in curbing its pain, hasn't it?"

"I have heard of instances where it's been prescribed by orthopedists." Andrews nodded as he stroked his chin.

"No further questions, Your Honor."

"Mr. Hawkins, you may call your next witness."

"The people call Miss Evelyn Wright, as a hostile witness," the district attorney said.

Murmurs in the courtroom.

The judge tapped his gavel.

Evelyn's blond hair was up in a bun. She wore heels, a charcoal dress below her knees, and a string of pearls. Everyone watched her as she made her way to the front of the courtroom and was sworn in.

"Ms. Wright, are you related to the defendant?" Hawkins said.

"Yes." She showed him her chiseled chin. "Alan is my brother."

"How often do you interact with each other in any given week?"

"Daily. We live in the same house."

"And you're also in charge of Dr. Wright's foundation?"

"That's correct."

"How frequently do you have business dealings with him?"

"Two or three times a week." Evelyn crossed her arms. "I have an office at Sunrise. We're building a pediatric wing to the hospital."

"Have you noticed any changes in him? A trembling hand when he's holding a fork, or maybe lack of focus during a discussion concerning the foundation?"

Evelyn's mouth formed a straight line.

A beat.

The judge leaned toward her.

"Ms. Wright, please remember you are under oath."

"I can't recall any specific instances."

"Have you ever gotten medication from the hospital for your brother?"

Evelyn glared at the district attorney. "Yes."

"Is this your signature?" Hawkins held a piece of paper in front of her.

She gave it a glance. "I believe it is."

"Did you ask your brother what this medication was for?"

"No."

"I would think being in charge of his foundation would

give you a fiduciary responsibility to know the status of his health. Isn't that correct?"

She shrugged. "That's not in the charter."

"Ladies and gentlemen of the jury." Hawkins held up a piece of paper. "I have here a copy of a ledger Evelyn Wright signed for anti-tremor medication that was prescribed to Alan Wright by Dr. Wright. It should be noted that it is legal in this state for a doctor to write himself a prescription for a non-opiate." Hawkins laid the ledger on the table. "We've been able to ascertain—through pharmaceutical companies and without breaking any HIPAA laws—that the defendant has prescribed this particular medication to his patients with LBD when they've had tremors. The date of Ms. Wright's signature is Friday, September 18, 2009. Two weeks before the accident that led to Cheryl Star's death—"

Wright sprang to his feet.

"I do have this disease!" There was a rumble of whispers throughout the room. "But I've never—"

"Dr. Wright, please sit down immediately and keep quiet, or you'll be removed from the courtroom."

When the bailiff started toward Wright's chair, he sat back down.

"Ms. Black, I'm giving you an hour to get your client under control," Markham said. "Then I want to see you and the district attorney in my chambers. Court dismissed for today."

CHAPTER 27

"Julian?" Julia clutched one of the bars that lined the side of her bed.

"I'm here."

The last time they'd made love was in Julia's childhood bedroom. Julia initiated it, peeling off her panties after sleeping next to him topless. It was early morning, the sun just creeping in. He hadn't expected it. A moment to hold on to. He wanted more—but now there was Richard, dead yet still between them.

"I'm dying." Julia's eyelids were half-closed.

"We all are," he said.

"I'm going sooner."

"There are still things we can try—"

"You're not a doctor." Julia wrinkled her forehead.

"And we're *not* giving up."

A young woman wearing a white dress wheeled a monitor into the room. An orderly with a tray of food entered behind her. Julian checked the wall clock.

"Enjoy your lunch." He waved. "See you later." He might not have forgiven her, but he'd never stop loving her. He had to try to save her.

———

Julian turned into Nellie's driveway, passing the simple wooden sign identifying the five-bedroom ranch as the Rubles'. Nellie's wife, Marie, was standing in the doorway.

"He's in the backyard, Julian."

He followed a stone path and found the neurologist on one knee, changing a lightbulb. He stood up and brushed himself off as Julian approached.

"Is it Julia?"

"It's Rig." Julian plopped into a lawn chair. "I don't think he can help her."

"He's the best neurosurgeon I know." Nellie sat next to him. "He operated on my uncle last year."

A dog howled. Julian looked up at a harvest moon. "There's got to be someone else," he said.

"No one I can think of that would be worth taking Rig off the case for." Nellie wiped his forehead with a handkerchief.

"What would you do?"

"Pray. Because right now she could use a miracle."

———

"Mr. Barnes, I'm afraid I'm out of options," Dr. Rig said.

"There's got to be something we can do." He leaned on Rig's mahogany desk.

"It's the location." He shook his head. "I'm sorry, truly I am. She seems like a special girl."

Julian stared into space, feeling hollow. "What about Alan Wright?"

"He *was* good." Rig's eyes pulled away. "In fact, I'd say the best I've ever seen."

"Couldn't you consult with him?"

"Mr. Barnes, he's on trial—"

"He's at home, Dr. Rig, with nothing to do but worry. Show him the scans, see what he thinks."

"It's unrealistic to think he—"

"Please, Doctor." Julian struggled to keep his voice level. "You said you were out of alternatives. Get his input. It's worth a shot."

———

"I need Wright's phone number, his home and e-mail addresses," Julian said.

"What are you going to do?" Tom was at his computer, typing something.

"Rig is out of options and Nelson doesn't know of anyone better. Wright's her best chance."

"With what he's going through . . ." Tom typed something else and clicked a button. "You really think he can come up with something?"

"I need to try."

"I hear you." Tom picked up a sheet of paper off the laser printer and handed it to him.

Julian took it and pulled out his cell phone. He had four bars. He started dialing.

"Hello," a woman's voice said after the fifth ring.

"Ms. Wright?"

"Yes."

"This is Julian Barnes. I was hoping to talk to your brother."

"Regarding what?"

"This has nothing to do with the trial." He figured it was best to make that clear right up front.

"Oh."

"My friend has a brain tumor."

There was a second of silence.

"You have the gall to call at this time, knowing what he must be going through? How could you be so insensitive?"

"Ms. Wright, she could die. I know what a genius Dr. Wright is. I can be there in an hour. Just let me talk to him. That's all I ask."

There was silence on the line.

"I'll do what I can." Evelyn sighed. "I can't make any promises. Alan's not in a good place—you are aware of that, aren't you?"

"Yes, and I appreciate your giving me the chance."

"Thank me after you see him."

———

It was dark and rainy, fog settling in. Julian's high beams reflected back at him. He turned them off. Not much better. He kept a watchful eye on the speedometer and wondered when car companies would start installing devices to warn drivers when they exceed the limit.

"Turn right here," the GPS lady said.

He slowed and got off the exit. He made a left at the end of the ramp and drove through a small town—diner, supermarket, hardware store, candle shop. He made his way along tree-lined streets with houses set back a good distance from the road.

There it was—105. He pulled into the driveway and stopped at a massive black gate. He opened his window and pushed a red button.

"Park in front of the house." Evelyn's voice came through the speaker. She sounded less hostile now.

The metal barrier crept up steadily as if to give the residents time to reconsider admitting their guests. Rain rattled his car's roof. He drove slowly on a long cobblestone driveway with lamplights on both sides that finally ended at a huge white Victorian house with a balcony wrapped around it as far as he could see. Evelyn stood near the door in tennis shoes, slacks, and a sweatshirt. Her hair was in a ponytail.

He made a run for it but still got drenched.

"I appreciate this," he said when he reached the top step soaking wet.

She waved him into a dark-paneled anteroom and handed him a thick white towel.

"Thanks." He ran it over his face and hair and handed it back to her.

"He's in the study." She started walking. "Follow me."

Ceiling lights reflected off the shiny hardwood floor of a long hallway.

Evelyn opened a door and walked in. Julian followed.

Wright was on a sofa, gazing at the fireplace through wire-rimmed glasses. Evelyn sat next to him and nodded to the chair on her right.

Julian sat. The crackling fire warmed his face. Evelyn's shoulder brushed Wright's. He didn't react. Julian twitched.

"Thank you for seeing me, Dr. Wright," he said.

A muscle momentarily protruded on Wright's jaw.

"Did Dr. Rig call you?" Julian's elbows were on his knees, clasped hands between them.

"I spoke to him briefly." Wright's lips barely moved. "The case is complicated."

"But you think there's a chance?"

"There might be."

"Your figuring it out is her only chance."

"It takes a lot of concentration, Mr. Barnes. I have other things on my mind. There are other good doctors out there."

"There's no one like you—we both know that." His heart raced as his mind searched for words that would convince him. "The other doctors are stumped." That had to appeal to him.

Wright was motionless. His glasses reflected the flames in front of him.

"At least look at the scans," Julian said. "I'll have Rig e-mail them to you."

Wright shook his head. "I can't right now."

"Sorry, Mr. Barnes." Evelyn had a hand on Wright's shoulder. "But I think it's better if you leave now."

"You still don't remember, do you?" Wright's gaze fixed on Julian.

"No memory." Julian stood up.

At least not anything relevant to the accident.

CHAPTER 28

Julian walked through Sunrise's parking lot, heading toward his car. He'd just seen Julia. She was feeling better, almost normal. Even if the tumor did grow back, it wouldn't be for a while. They could have a few months of pretending things were fine.

But he couldn't. His heart was numb. He needed time they didn't have.

Would he really let himself lose her? He couldn't imagine doing that. If Wright *did* operate and save her, could he resume their relationship? As if she hadn't cheated on him? He couldn't imagine that, either.

His cell rang. "Wright pled guilty to involuntary manslaughter, second degree," Tom said.

"He's going to jail?" Julian switched the phone from one hand to the other.

"He'll be in minimum security and out in two years on good behavior. Doubt he'll ever practice medicine again, though—hold on, this is interesting."

"What?"

"Wright made a statement. He maintains his innocence, says that due to certain circumstantial evidence against him he currently can't counter, he's been left with no choice but to plead to a lesser charge."

"*Currently* could mean they have a plan to eventually exonerate him." Julian stared at the sky. Stars twinkled. A plane crossed above him. He breathed in the cool air and pictured Wright sitting in a jail cell.

It felt wrong. All wrong.

"Hello." A familiar voice from behind him.

He turned around. It was Evelyn.

"I've got to go." Julian dropped his cell into the case clipped to his belt.

"Picking up some of Alan's things." She put a covered cardboard box down on the ground.

"I won't keep you." He produced his car keys. "I'm sure you need to get back to your brother."

"His assistant is covering for me." She tilted her head back. "It's a clear night. All the stars are out." She pointed to the sky. "And look at that moon. Complete. Full." She took in a deep breath and let it out.

His stomach growled. "Excuse me." He patted his belly. "I haven't had dinner."

"Neither have I." She cupped her elbow with one hand,

supported her chin with the other. "There's a good upscale diner near here."

"The Athenian?"

"Yes."

He always passed it on the way to visit Julia in the hospital. He'd never been in it.

"Let's go together." She opened the trunk and put the box in it. The lid closed automatically. "Leave your car here. I'll drive."

"Really?" he said. "You and I break bread after what we've been through?"

"I've got an idea."

"You do?" He was intrigued. Still, he had to be careful. She couldn't possibly have his best interest at heart.

"I think it's a good idea and I'd like to act quickly. We shouldn't waste the opportunity."

"What's this about?"

"I'll tell you over dinner. Let's go." She patted her stomach. "I'm hungry, too."

He got into her red Audi, which smelled of leather. He could barely hear the engine as they left the lot.

"I don't have a lot of vices, Mr. Barnes, but sports cars are one of them." She pressed down on the accelerator and the vehicle surged forward. Julian cyed the speedometer—she was dead on the limit. "I just don't like to drive them fast."

He looked out the windshield and checked on the moon. Evelyn had said it was full. He wished he could find at least a sliver that was eclipsed. Some astronomical defect in the scene above. But there was none—the moon was perfectly round against a black sky, and he was sitting in Evelyn's car, about to have dinner with her.

He watched the street scenes they passed and enjoyed the Audi's smooth ride.

The light ahead of them turned green. Evelyn started through the intersection. A black SUV came from the left, running the light. She slammed on the brakes, the car jerked to a halt, and the momentum thrust them forward like crash-test dummies.

"Whoa." Evelyn swiped her forehead with the back of her hand. "That was close. Just another second or two and—"

Remember.

He's in his car. Going faster, heading toward an intersection.

"You okay?" Evelyn shook him.

"I . . . I guess I was—"

"Back at that night?"

"No." He rubbed his temple. "I mean, maybe. Yes. I'm not sure."

"It must be terrible for you, not being able to remember."

"It is."

"Do you want to talk about it?" Her stare seemed scrutinizing.

"Thanks . . . but I'd rather not."

"Just know that I'd listen." She touched his arm lightly. His spine rattled—there was something off about her. But hadn't he thought that for a long time? What bothered him even more was that he didn't know what it was.

Her car soon ascended a ramp to the parking lot for the Athenian, a one-story building with big windows so dark they obliterated any view of its patrons.

"So nice to see you, Ms. Wright," a chubby maître d' with jet-black hair and a short neat beard said as soon as they were inside.

A dessert case had cakes, cookies, and pastries on display. Evelyn held on to the glass counter as if to steady herself.

"Are you okay?" Julian's hand hovered near her elbow, ready to catch her.

"Yes. Thanks. Just a balance problem." She smiled. "Alberto, I hadn't expected to see you here."

"It didn't work out." He removed a white cloth from his jacket pocket and patted his forehead with it. "I'm back for good."

"This is Julian Barnes." Evelyn turned toward him.

"Hello, Mr. Barnes." Alberto extended his fleshy hand. "Nice to meet you. Is it your first time here?"

"Yes." He surveyed the area. The counters shone. So did the marble floor. The walls had tasteful paintings of colonnades, coliseums, and Hellenistic sculptures. "I look forward to trying your food."

"I'm sure you'll be pleased." Alberto smiled broadly. He had big white teeth. His gaze went toward Evelyn. "Isn't that right, Ms. Wright?"

"He selects only the best cuts of meat." She elbowed the maître d'. "Could we have our table in the back?"

"Follow me." Alberto led them on a tile floor that gave way

to thick carpeting as the lighting grew dimmer. They stopped next to a two-person table. The chairs were big, with generous cushions.

Julian and Evelyn sat across from one another and were each handed a huge spiral-bound, laminated menu.

"Would you like a martini?" Alberto's hands were clasped in front of him.

"Yes." Evelyn looked at Julian. He held up two fingers. He'd nurse one.

"Coming right up. William will be right over." Alberto turned and left.

Julian was looking at a couple not far from their table—a man in his mid-fifties with a ravishing redhead, mid-thirties—when William returned with two martinis.

"Are you ready to order?"

"I'll have the usual," Evelyn said.

"The same." Julian assumed it wasn't vegetarian.

"Coming right up."

Julian sipped his drink. The vodka stung his throat, soothed his insides, and made him feel lighter.

"Do you have siblings?" Evelyn had already put a good dent in her martini.

"A brother." He found he didn't even want to tell her that much.

"We have that in common. Do you and . . ."

"Tom."

"Do you and *Tom* keep in touch?" She uttered his brother's name as if savoring having extracted it from him.

"Yes and no."

"It sounds like you two have an understanding."

"We don't have high expectations of what our relationship should be, so we're happy with what we have."

She stirred her drink. The liquid swirled in the glass, mesmerizing him.

"Do you have many friends?" she said.

"No."

"Neither do I." Her blue eyes brightened. "It's really just Alan and me." She lowered her gaze. "My father died of an aneurysm. It was at the dinner table. Alan was standing next to me, holding my hand, telling me not to look as the paramedics worked on our father, but I couldn't stop."

"That must've been traumatic."

"It was, especially for Alan. He's sensitive." Her chest rose. "That's why I need to protect him."

"I see." He tried to sound nonchalant.

"Our mother passed not long after our dad."

"What happened to her? If you don't mind my asking."

"She fell . . . down the basement stairs and broke her neck." Evelyn sipped more of her drink. "Alan and I became even closer after we lost our parents. Blood is a very special bond, Mr. Barnes." She leaned toward him, a hint of alcohol on her breath. "Your meeting with Alan rejuvenated him."

"Really?" He pictured Wright staring at the fire, barely moving. "I didn't get that impression."

"Things aren't always as they seem." She shook her head slowly. "He never turns anyone away. He works until he finds a solution. And they want to put him in jail." She sighed. "He was working this morning. It's helping him. He's more talkative, more himself, despite the dreadful circumstances." She showed him a fist. "We Wrights are fighters. Alan seemed to lose that for a while. It's good to see it back."

"Do you know what he was working on?" His stomach felt weightless, ready to plummet.

"Rig sent him the scans." She looked at him as if she couldn't understand why he'd ask her such an inane question.

"Evelyn, I—"

"I know you want to save her," she said. "My Alan is your only chance. The problem is he's going to prison. Can you conceive of a society so dysfunctional it incarcerates a man of his prowess and stature? It's absurd."

The waiter came and put sizzling meat in front of each of them, and after he was assured they needed nothing further, he spun around and attended to the couple across from them.

"It's their New York strip steak." Evelyn's eyes were closed, nostrils positioned over her meal. "It smells delicious."

"It does." Julian inhaled, took in the scent.

"Alan is studying Julia's case as we speak." Evelyn sprinkled salt on her steak. "He's already made some progress." She impaled a chunk of meat with her fork, cut off a hunk, and put it in her mouth. "He's going in a different direction," she said when she'd finally stopped chewing and swallowed.

"How so?"

"My brother thinks broadly. You'd be surprised how many of his peers don't. Alan has grown exponentially as a surgeon, particularly these past few years. But he can't help Julia from jail."

"I understand that." Julian put down his utensils. "What is it you want?"

"Say you remember." Her voice softened, her tone convincing. "Tell them you ran the light."

Now his stomach fell, leaving him feeling queasy. Of course, he'd had the same idea. But what about Cough?

"Even though I don't know if I did."

"It's what's best for everyone." She sounded totally confident. "I'd do it for Alan in a heartbeat." She gave him that look again. The one that said he was a fool for not seeing what was so obvious. "It'll save Julia's life. Think about it."

"I have."

Julian saw himself prostrate in front of Judge Markham, confessing to a crime he wasn't sure he'd committed. The Stars look at him with disgust. What was a few years of his life compared with the rest of Julia's? Even if they didn't end up together, he loved her enough to do that for her. But—

Don't remember or Julia dies.

He and Tom had to find Cough and make sure he couldn't hurt Julia. With Slattery's help, they could do that. They had to.

"Tell him I'll do it," Julian said. "If he can come up with a cure."

"I'll call you as soon as he has a solution. It shouldn't be much longer." She looked up, to her right. "Whatever happened with that person who threatened you?"

"That still needs to be resolved."

"Mr. Barnes, I have resources that might help in that area, if it means securing your confession and keeping Alan out of jail." She lowered her eyes. "I know I wasn't forthcoming when we spoke about it initially, and I apologize for that."

"Why the sudden change?" He leaned over the table toward her.

"At the time, your failure to remember was an obstacle." She raised her chin. "It was creating a frustrating situation for us, and I admit I took some of that anger out on you."

"Okay . . ."

"But don't you see? Now we can make this work in our favor by ensuring our stories coincide, securing Alan's freedom."

"That's . . . an interesting perspective." He'd never trusted her. Now he knew he'd been right.

"I'm good at coming up with creative solutions." Evelyn rested her folded hands on the edge of the table. He noticed them trembling. "And I do whatever it takes to get the results I want."

He leaned back, just a little. "You've made that abundantly clear."

CHAPTER 29

*T*he brothers were rocking their chairs on Tom's front porch. The sun shone bright in a vibrant blue sky. Rebel and Buzz were off somewhere. It was just the two of them. Julian's sip from the mug of coffee Tom had given him singed his throat. He blew on it and waited for it to cool.

"Evelyn had an idea," he said. "It might be Julia's only chance."

"Oh?" Tom had one eye on him. "This should be interesting."

"She wants me to say I'm guilty."

"Huh?"

"I say I ran the light, Wright is freed, and he operates on Julia."

"She wants you to do this even though you *don't* remember?" Tom flared his nostrils.

"Freeing Wright is the only way to save Julia."

"You don't know that for sure! What are you, crazy?"

"I'm desperate."

"You'd be in prison."

"For two years."

"That's Wright's sentence—you might get a longer one. He's a sick man who made a mistake. You'd be seen as reckless and could end up spending years behind bars for a crime you didn't commit!"

"We don't know that. And Julia is facing a death sentence."

"Lying to a judge." Tom peered at him. "You could do that?"

"It wouldn't be easy." He was sweating just thinking about it. "But the stakes are high enough."

"You could be jailed for obstruction of justice."

"Come on, Tom, surely you see the merit in this?"

"First off, Wright has to come up with a cure."

"I made that a condition of my confession. And Evelyn seems to think it's imminent. She said he was 'moving in a different direction,' whatever that means."

Tom sighed. "Julian, I'll be there for you no matter what, but this is a bad idea. There's too much risk on your part. And if Cough makes good on his threat—"

"Stopping Cough is still the first priority."

"At least we agree on something," Tom said.

"Let's concentrate on Cough and deal with Evelyn's idea later."

"I'm okay with that." Tom sat back in his seat. "What's next?"

"I want to talk to Store, one-on-one. Maybe he's not Cough, but maybe I'm not the only one who's been threatened. Do you know where he is?"

"Give me a minute." Tom took out his cell. His finger played on its screen. "His car is up by his cabin in Stratford Falls."

"Perfect." Julian preferred a secluded location.

"He may not be Cough, but we know he has a gun permit. He *could* still be dangerous."

"I agree. A little precaution wouldn't be a mistake."

———

Julian's pulse was racing when Tom pulled off the road and onto the dirt shoulder. A light rain fell. Drops dotted the windshield. The sky was thick with gray clouds.

Tom opened the glove compartment, reached in, and took out a pistol. Julian shrank from it.

"Take it," Tom said.

"That thing still works?" He let his fingers wrap the handle and remembered the times he and Tom shot cans in their backyard. Most days Tom won. Still, Julian always managed a respectable score.

"It shoots as well as the last time you used it," Tom said.

Julian checked the barrel. Empty.

Tom dropped six bullets into his palm.

"You won't use these, but it'll be good to have them."

He inserted the first bullet, his stomach on edge, fingers unsteady. Tom watched him intensely. Julian missed the hole completely with the second bullet. It landed on the floorboard and rolled of sight.

His fingertips scraped dirt and sand as they searched until he finally retrieved the bullet and finished loading the weapon without further incident. All the while, Tom's eyes were on him.

Julian activated the safety. Tom handed him a holster. It had two straps. Julian pulled up his pant leg and tied the top one tight around his calf and the lower just above his ankle. He made sure both were secure, sheathed the pistol in the leather case, and let his pant leg fall. Tom retrieved his M14 from the backseat. It had an infrared scope and a bipod.

"Now let me take one last look at that wire."

Julian lifted his shirt.

"That's better." Tom pressed the adhesive strip down and Julian winced—a remnant from the accident. "Sorry."

"That's okay. Go on."

After Tom finished, Julian took out his cell and started dialing.

Store picked up on the third ring. "Who are you and what do you want from me?" He slurred the words. Julian recalled the veins on Store's nose when he was on the witness stand. Maybe from over-imbibing?

"Mr. Store, this is Julian Barnes."

"The other driver."

"Yes. I'm at the foot of your driveway. I'd like to talk to you."

"About what?"

"I'm going to tell them the accident was my fault." He'd reveal no more than that.

"Why would you?"

"It's the truth." He figured this was as good a time as any to practice lying. "You're mistaken about what you saw."

"Mr. Barnes, he's guilty." Cough. "He thinks he's above everything, including the law. He'll do whatever he can to wiggle out of this. What's he offering you?"

"He's not. I—"

"Doesn't matter. Didn't expect you to answer anyway. I wouldn't if I were in your shoes. I'm on my front porch. Let's talk." Store hung up.

"You heard?" Julian said.

"All of it." Tom pointed. "There's a rise over there. It'll give me a clear line of sight to the front of the cabin." He looked through binoculars. "Store *is* on the porch." Tom stuck a bud in his ear and spun a dial on a tiny electronic component. "If this microphone can do what the manufacturer claims, I'll hear everything."

They got out of the truck.

"I'll be watching." Tom tapped his ear. "And listening."

———

The air was dank. Drizzle dampened Julian's hair and dotted his duffle coat. The holster was tight around his ankle. His feet squished mud, which rose over the edges of his sneakers. He leaped to avoid what looked like another soft patch and landed on a twig. *Snap.* He imagined diving for refuge behind a boulder as bullets blew by his skull.

He continued toward the figure on the front porch, a man sitting at a table. Julian's senses tingled, every cell alert.

"Hello, Mr. Barnes," Store said.

Julian glanced at a window. A light was on. Maybe someone was inside?

"Care for some whiskey?" Store held up a bottle by its neck.

"No, thanks." He remembered Cough's voice all too well. "You're not him, are you?"

"Who did you think I might be?" Store cocked any eyebrow.

"Someone who threatened me if I remember the accident."

"Sure you don't mind a little whiskey?" Store shoved the bottle toward him.

"Okay. I'll try some." Julian had to admit, Store was being hospitable.

"Good." With a disturbing intensity, Store half-filled a glass with a brown liquid. "I haven't threatened anyone. Nor has anyone threatened me. I've been spared that." He picked up a pair of tongs and dropped two cubes into the glass. "Though I'm not surprised someone is willing to inflict harm to keep the truth from coming out. The stakes are certainly high enough." He handed him his drink. "I wouldn't be surprised if Wright and/or the sister were behind these shenanigans. They'd do anything to save themselves. Marcy's cover-up proves that."

After taking a sip, Julian shifted the glass from one hand to the other, fearing the alcohol might impair his reflexes.

"I'm telling the truth about what I saw that night." Store's fingertips shook. "You can't take the fall for him. No amount of money is worth that."

"Maybe I should go." This man was in pain. Julian didn't need to exacerbate it.

"I've been following Wright since Marcy died."

Julian froze.

"Not all the time." Store's eyes were jaundiced, his breath pungent. "But always when I heard Marcy's voice." Cough. "There was a playground I'd take her to when she was a little girl. She'd spread her arms and scream as she ran toward the entrance." He wiped a tear with the heel of his hand. "The same scream every time. Funny how kids can do things like that." He shook his head slowly. "My Marcy. I miss her."

Julian crafted the scene in his mind. He found it easy to picture the pride and love Store must have experienced. Now, that memory must be agony.

"Some days, I would take her just to hear her scream." A tear gathered at the corner of Store's eyes and spilled over. "I never told her that. I wish I had. But since she died, whenever I heard her make that sound of joy in my head, I'd pack a gun and follow him. The first time, I almost did it. Funny, it was one of the best opportunities I had. Probably *the* best. Don't get me wrong, there've been others. But this was perfect. He was coming out of Sunrise. It was late at night and no one was around. He was right in front of me. All I had to do was stick the gun in his back and pull the trigger. One bullet to the spine. That would've satisfied me." He held his thumb and index fingers barely apart. "I was this close, but I couldn't do it. Kept following him, though. I had other times, like I said. But I could never bring myself to pull the trigger." He sighed. "Wright would've saved her."

"What happened exactly?" Julian whispered.

"Marcy had a blood clot in her brain." Store grabbed the whiskey bottle and emptied what was left of its contents into his glass. "Wright was going to do the procedure. The nurses told us how lucky we were to have their top neurosurgeon on such short notice."

Store took a gulp of whiskey. Julian took a sip.

"Everything was fine until the paramedics brought in a man with a brain injury." It was a minute before Store could go on. "He'd been shot in the head by the police—he robbed a bank and killed a guard. Wright operated on him instead." Store took another swallow of his drink. "They said Marcy died from a reaction to the anesthesia, but do you know the odds of that?"

Julian shook his head.

"Two hundred thousand to one. And that's on the low side. I left the hospital in a stupor. Couldn't drive. I walked home, sat in my living room, had a whiskey, and pondered things. Went back to the hospital a few days later and saw this guy in personnel. Crenshaw. Seemed nice. He said he'd look into the situation and get back to me. I thought I'd get some answers. Instead, Crenshaw calls me back, tells me everything was *copacetic.* Actually used that word. I knew then if I wanted justice, I had to get it myself."

BRRING. A phone rang once. Store paid no attention to it.

"Wright is guilty." Store smiled slightly. "All that time following him and it paid off—just not the way I had expected. It was good seeing him on trial. And now I know he'll die slow. That sentence he'll never overturn." He finished off his drink. "It was hard after Marcy died. Then Beth got this lump, and by the time she had a mammogram it was too late."

He pictured Julia lying on a gurney. Was it too late for her?

"Last week, I go to my doctor with back pain." Store coughed. "They run a bunch of tests and diagnose me with bladder cancer. They think they can cure it with chemo, but I've had enough." He surveyed the area. "There's nothing left here for me."

That's when Julian saw a barrel by Store's thigh.

Store produced the pistol and pointed it at Julian.

"Get the hell out of here!" he screamed.

Julian bolted. He was halfway up the driveway when he heard the shot.

His bones shook from the explosion. His eyes snapped shut. He heard metal crumble, glass shattering. Felt the seat belt knife his shoulder. He'd run out of Julia's apartment, gotten in his car, and made a bet with fate.

If he got through the intersection without stopping, he wouldn't lose Julia.

He remembered.

CHAPTER 30

*T*om had already come down from the overlook by the time the shot was fired, but not quickly enough to stop Julian from seeing Store's dead body. They'd driven back to Tom's cabin in silence.

Now Tom pulled into his driveway and cut the engine. The wipers stopped. He leaned against the headrest. Rain and perspiration dotted his forehead.

"I remembered." Julian's heart was easily over a hundred beats a minute. "I made a bet with fate. You remember doing that when we were kids?"

"Yeah." Tom twirled the toothpick in his mouth. "What did you wager?"

"If I got through the intersection without stopping, I wouldn't lose her."

"Go on."

"I saw Julia . . . in her bedroom . . . with someone else."

"What'd you do?" Tom's eyes were wide.

"I ran out of there, got in my car, and started driving. That's when I made the bet. The signal was green as I approached the intersection, was still green when I reached it. I thought *I won't lose her.* Then Wright T-boned me."

"And the light?"

"Green." Julian took a deep breath. "Wright ran the light."

"Maybe he *thought* it was green," Tom said.

"The Lewy body dementia? Maybe."

Tom opened the door and left the truck. Julian followed. Rebel barked, came up to him, and licked his hand.

"Good boy. Make nice to your uncle." Tom patted the dog's head. "He needs all the love he can get right now."

An owl hooted. Julian was free—though maybe not for much longer.

"I'm pouring us a drink," Tom said when they were inside. "But first I'm getting us dry clothes."

"I could use both of those." He unbuttoned his shirt. The collar was damp.

"Be right back."

Julian extracted himself from his muddy sneakers. His socks were soaked. He sneezed.

———

Julian wore a gray sweatshirt and faded jeans, both a size too big. Tom had washed Julian's sneakers and they were drying by the fire. A mild scent of burning rubber wafted from that direction.

"You smell that?" he said.

Tom took a whiff.

"It's sneaker sole. They'll be fine. I do it all the time." Tom knelt by the wooden coffee table and filled two shot glasses with tequila. He handed Julian one and picked up the other. Julian downed the shot. Tom did, too.

"One more." Tom started pouring.

"I might not be able to do this for a while." He relished the warmth filling his body.

"You weren't speeding when you breached the intersection?" Tom handed him another drink.

"No, that would have affected the result." Julian took the glass. "Then it's not up to fate and the bet is meaningless."

"So that stoplight analysis was flawed." Tom sat across from him on the couch. Hands behind his head.

"Temperature *can* affect the light's switch mechanism. They collected their data during a cold snap in February. It was balmy the night of the accident. Also, the light had been repaired, so the equipment they tested wasn't the exact same in use at the time the accident occurred. All in the details. That's why they say the devil's there." Julian had a recollection. "I need to talk to Slattery about that."

"You're innocent and willing to go to jail." Tom grimaced and picked up his drink. "To save the woman who cheated on you."

"As soon as we deal with Cough."

"Absolutely. That goes without saying. We deal with Cough before you do anything."

"Good thing I didn't drink much at—" Julian smacked his forehead. "Wait . . . I touched a glass at Store's."

"We've got to go get it." Tom grabbed his boots and stepped into them. "You don't want something like that out there."

"My only connection to Store." He seized his sneakers from the fire. They were almost dry—a pleasant surprise.

"No loose ends." Tom tied his shoelaces. "Now let's go get that glass."

———

Store had fallen backward in his chair, arms and legs sprawled, lips turned up slightly. His grip released from the gun, revealing a mother-of-pearl handle. Julian empathized, felt the depth of his loneliness, the pain of losing the people who mattered.

Now he stared at the winding country road as Tom's truck hummed toward Store's cabin. He'd once watched a documentary about life in a prison and knew it would be hard. That first morning in particular, feeling like he'd been kicked in the gut when he opens his eyes and realizes where he'll be until they decide to set him free.

Tom pulled onto the shoulder and came to a halt. After turning off the lights, he reached under his seat and pulled out a pair of infrared binoculars.

"Up here Store might not be found for days," Tom said. "We could use a place to park."

"There's a scenic overlook." Julian pointed to a blue sign with an arrow.

"That'll work." Tom turned into a space perpendicular to the road. "Do you have your cell?"

"Yeah." He had it clipped to his belt. Reception had two bars, the battery one. He made a mental note to charge it.

"Keep an eye out." Tom held the door's handle. "I've got my phone on 'vibrate.'"

"I should go." Julian reached for the door handle. "I was there."

"You're probably still in shock. I can do this—it's no big deal. Really."

"Okay." He slumped back in his seat. "Thank you."

"It's what brothers are for. You put the glass on the table next to his?"

"Yes." He visualized doing that. "Store's glass was almost empty, mine almost full."

"Got it. Be right back." Tom got out of the truck and closed the door behind him.

Julian watched him go down the road until he disappeared at the entrance.

Silence.

A moment of peace. There might not be many more of these, not for a while. How long would he be in prison? Tom had said he might not get Wright's sentence. He couldn't tell them about his bet with fate   they'd perceive him as reckless, slap him with a longer sentence.

Out the window, a black sedan moved in and out of the glow of a street lamp, its red rear lights the last thing he saw before it vanished around a bend.

A rap on the window startled him. He checked the driver's window and clicked open the locks.

Tom got into the truck, shut the door, and turned on the ignition.

"No glass," he said.

"How can that be?"

Tom shrugged. "Everything else looks to be just the way it was."

"This can't be good."

"There's nothing we can do about it. Besides, when they do find Store, I'm sure they'll call it a suicide. That aspect of the crime scene seemed untouched." Tom backed the truck out of the parking space and turned right. He drove past Store's house. A light fog hung over the place.

"Still quiet," Julian said as they went by. After a mile on the same road, a car came toward them in the distance. Red and orange lights rotated on its roof.

Getting closer. Julian heard noise—a siren.

A cop car. It sped past, siren screaming, ambulance tailing it.

"You think they're going to Store's?" Julian looked at the two vehicles from over his shoulder.

"There's one way to find out." Tom slowed and made a right. He drove up a road with large houses on either side. The truck went higher. The houses got nicer. Still higher—the engine revved, complaining. There was another scenic overlook. He pulled into it, kept the car running, and got out.

Julian stood next to him.

Below them the police cruiser and the ambulance were parked at Store's. An officer was cordoning off the area with yellow crime-scene tape.

"Whoever took the glass must've called it in," Julian said.

"Seems logical." Tom nodded.

A muscled officer stood at the foot of Store's driveway, head bobbing.

"They have everything they need to figure out what happened." Tom played with his missing goatee. "No crime was committed, and the glass has been disposed of."

"We just don't know who took it or why." His stomach somersaulted at the thought of someone having such incriminating evidence on him. It made him feel exposed, naked.

"Let's get out of here," Tom said.

They hustled back to the truck.

"Can you research Melvin?" Julian buckled his seat belt.

"The maintenance man? Sure." Tom started the motor. "Why?"

"He's the one who put me on to Store." Julian stared out the window. "Maybe his motive wasn't as altruistic as I once thought."

CHAPTER 31

"Melvin Winters has worked in a number of cleaning positions over the past dozen years." Tom was making omelets. His culinary creations could evoke rapture as long as he didn't get *too* creative.

Julian sat at the kitchen table and took notes.

"Melvin's stint at Sunrise has been the longest." Tom turned the knob on the burner. The flame rose. "Two years."

"Melvin wasn't there when Marcy died?" He hadn't expected that.

"Nope." Tom opened a cabinet, reached up, and came down with a big blue bowl.

"He lied." Julian thought back. "He sounded convincing at the time."

"He's done some acting—not just local theater but a couple of Off-Broadways. Got that off his Facebook page."

"Now, that's interesting."

"Melvin was arrested when he was eighteen. He hasn't had an altercation with the law since." Tom cracked an egg. He let the contents tumble into the bowl and tossed the shattered shell into the garbage. "He has twenty thousand in credit card debt and a six-fifty credit score."

"He set us up." Julian was pissed.

"Or someone egged him on." Tom beat the contents of the bowl. "Pun intended."

"The trick is getting him to talk."

"I know his social, bank, and credit card numbers." Tom poured the whipped eggs into the frying pan. They slightly sizzled and soon firmed. "We can hit him electronically."

"I'd like to try to reason with him first."

———

A breeze fondled Julian's face as he and Tom stood across the street from the rear entrance to Sunrise Hospital. According to Tom, Melvin's shift had just ended.

The service door opened and Melvin stepped out and turned right on the sidewalk. He hurried down the block, hands in his brown uniform's trouser pockets. Julian followed him from the opposite side of the street, head lowered, using parked cars as shields. After a block, he crossed the road and got in front of Melvin.

Melvin stopped. They were face-to-face.

"What do you want?" Melvin said.

"I need your help."

"Excuse me. You're blocking my path." Melvin had cigarette smoke on his breath and looked heftier than Julian remembered.

"You weren't at Sunrise when Marcy died." Julian's voice was monotone. "You lied about that."

"I didn't lie about what happened."

"Who put you up to it? Was it Evelyn? You didn't plan this yourself."

"It happened. That's all you should be concerned with." He went by him and resumed walking.

Julian tried to keep up with him, but when Melvin broke into a jog, Julian halted.

"We both know there's more to it than that." Julian watched Melvin shrink into the distance.

A blue double-decker bus pulled to the curb ahead of Melvin. Its doors retracted. Melvin scaled its stairs and disappeared like he'd been swallowed.

The double-decker surged away from the sidewalk. The bus gained so much momentum as it came toward Julian that for an instant he thought Melvin had managed to persuade the driver to mow him down. Julian stepped back onto the curb as the bus whisked by, giving off fierce fumes as it rolled down the broad boulevard.

Melvin appeared in the rear bay window, showing Julian his middle finger, then the back of his head. The bus moved out of sight shortly after that.

Melvin knew something, but threats weren't going to

extract it from him—not even the electronic variety. Julian was now certain of that.

———

Julian dialed a number. "I remembered," he said after Slattery picked up.

"The whole thing?"

"It all came back to me last night." He left it at that for the present. Given his lack of proficiency as a liar, the less he said the better. "Wright is guilty."

"I'm not completely surprised. This morning I took a closer look at the stoplight analysis. It was by no means the slam dunk I thought it was. Should've reviewed it sooner." He sounded frustrated. "It was a rookie mistake. I'm usually more buttoned down than that."

"Stuff happens. No hard feelings here." He just wished Slattery hadn't put him through that while he and Julia were on vacation.

"Alan *should* be going to jail," Slattery said.

"He might not be."

"Why, what did you hear?"

"So you're not aware of *her* plan?" He found it easy to imagine tension between Evelyn and Slattery.

"Whose plan?"

"Evelyn's."

"That's news to me. I work for Dr. Wright and *only* Dr. Wright. I do have some information I want to share with you, though. Can you and Tom stop by later? We'll have dessert and compare notes."

"Sure. I've got some facts you'll find interesting."

"Good." Then Slattery surprised him. "Right now I'm at the hospital and need your auditing expertise."

"I'll try to help." It had been a while. His skills might be rusty.

"I'm in Sunrise's Accounts Payable department. The supervisor is gone for the day and her assistant called in sick. How would I research a payment without accessing a computer?"

"How far back are you going?"

"Last year," Slattery said.

"Do you know who the vendor is?"

"No, but I might know the name if I see it."

"You need the vendor reports." He recalled the last time he'd used them, auditing a crystal-exporting firm. "They're usually bound computer printouts kept chronologically. There's a summary and a detail. Start with the summary. You should find an alphabetical section. Once you locate the vendor, copy their number and look it up in the detail report."

"Let me make a note of that," Slattery said. "Okay, please continue."

"The vendor detail contains a record of all transactions for the time period of that report. They'll probably be in voucher-number sequence, which, if you're lucky, there's a hard copy of in the vicinity."

"I noticed a bunch of metal filing cabinets marked 'vouchers' on the way in."

"That should be what you're looking for."

"Sounds doable," Slattery said. "Let me just go over my notes one more time." Silence on the line. "Think I got it. Thanks."

"Hope it helps." He didn't ask what Slattery was up to. Hopefully, he'd hear about it when they met.

"You'll be the first to know if I come up with anything," Slattery said.

———

Julian entered Tom's office, hoping Slattery had found whatever he was after. Tom was seated behind his computer with headphones around his neck, hands clasped behind his head. Julian sat on the couch.

"Did you hear a cell phone ring when you were at Store's?" Tom said.

"I heard a phone ring. It sounded like an old-fashioned telephone."

"A lot of cell users have it. Could be someone who pines for the good old days." Tom played the sound: *BRRING*.

"That's it. But it only rang once."

"Which means someone could've silenced it."

"In the meantime, we'd better get going or we'll be late for our meeting with Slattery."

CHAPTER 32

Julian and Tom sat in Slattery's dining room with a plate of cannolis on the round oak table. A Tiffany lamp hung above it.

"I think this bakery makes the best I've ever had." Slattery jutted his pinky at the three different sizes of the pastry. "Try one of each." He took a reflective bite of the largest one.

Julian's hand jittered as he sipped some java. It was dark and strong. The coffee in prison must be like water. He'd have to get used to doing with less—much less. And maybe for a long time.

"Julian, lying in a murder investigation is obstruction of justice." Slattery had on a white shirt, no tie, sleeves neatly folded up, top two buttons open. "There's a judge on trial for it. He's looking at doing some serious time."

"Julia's life is at stake."

"Yours could be, too." Slattery eyed Julian. "Store's dead. Committed suicide."

"When?" Tom did a good job of sounding surprised.

"Last night." Slattery dabbed his lips with a napkin. "It'll be on the evening news."

Julian sat stone-faced, wondering how much Slattery knew.

"I think I figured out who Cough is," Slattery said.

"We're listening." Julian sat up.

"This will take a while." Slattery stretched his arms above his head. "I'll start from the beginning."

"My favorite place." Tom grinned.

"A PI was on Store the day he came forward as a witness." Slattery propped up his chin. "That's pretty much standard industry practice with criminal-case clients these days. The investigator the Wrights' law firm hired, Xander Sousa, notes in his initial investigation that Store coughed when under pressure. The report also mentions Store's wife had recently died of cancer and that she had salt-and-pepper hair."

"So who's on the distribution list for that report?" Tom said.

"I'm getting to that." As Slattery finished the last of his cannoli, the pleasure on his face quickly faded. "I had a productive day at Sunrise." He brushed white powder off his hands. "The first thing I did was show up unannounced at Evelyn's office. I wanted to ask her a few questions, catch her off guard, observe her reactions." He reached for another pastry but jerked his hand away. "Well, I get there and her door was closed. A buffer was in a corner next to it."

"She and Melvin?" Julian said.

"Yep. So I went down to the lockers and found Melvin's. He had one of those combination locks. Like the ones in high school?"

Julian and Tom nodded.

"Got it open on the very first try." Slattery buffed his nails on his shirt. "Good to know I still got the touch."

"Don't tell me you found a wig?" Tom said.

"That would've been too easy. There was only his jacket and some hair spray. So when that turned out to be a bust, I went to Accounts Payable to see if I came up with any fishy payments."

"Worth a shot." Tom bit into his cannoli. Julian had no appetite.

"Julian gave me good guidance." Slattery flipped a notebook page. "One of their vendors is Abracadabra. The name piqued my curiosity, and when it said they were set up in October 2009, I was intrigued. 'Costume store' was in the description. No surprise there, since the staff occasionally puts on a play for the children's wing. I've attended one myself. Still, I checked the payment history and found one on 10/9/09 for ten thousand dollars, and it turns out their address is the same as Melvin's."

Julian felt rage roil inside him.

"My guess is when you contracted amnesia," Slattery said, "Evelyn conceived the idea for Cough and hired Melvin to play the part. But then Cough became an impediment after she decided to make a deal with Julian and have him claim to remember."

"That's why she offered to help with Cough," Julian said. "Not initially, but later on."

"You never would've heard from the Coughster again." Tom guffawed.

"Sounds like she was definitely doing damage control." Slattery snickered.

"I thought it was a little too easy getting into Sunrise's record retention," Tom said. "They wanted us to find out about Store."

"Evelyn has a lot of pull at that hospital and isn't afraid to use it," Slattery said. "She could've gotten a few select staff members at Sunrise to participate in the charade without citing too many specifics."

"Even if that's true, it doesn't change anything," Julian said. "We need to work with her to free Wright so he can save Julia."

"So Evelyn gets away with it?" Tom's eyes were immense.

"For now." Slattery rolled down his shirt sleeves and buttoned them. "I have a meeting with the coroner, John McKenna. I'm looking forward to his reactions when we discuss the mistake on his report."

"I'll do some digging," Tom said. "See what I can find on him."

"Good." Slattery said. "Julian, you look exhausted. Get some rest."

———

"Come on." Tom headed toward his office. Julian followed him. "Let's see what we can find on Mr. McKenna." Tom sat at his desk and started typing.

Julian was across from him, slouched in a chair. His arms felt heavy.

"Shoot," Tom said. "The hospital system is down. They must have a snap server I can get into. Give me a second." His fingers moved furiously. Tom once said he could do a hundred twenty words a minute. "Okay, I'm in now." A blip. He was reading, light from the screen reflected off his face. "Interesting."

"What is?" Julian's eyelids felt massive.

"We should show this to Slattery before he talks to McKenna." Tom looked up from the screen. "Julian, you okay?"

"Slattery was right—I'm exhausted." And woozy. "Need to rest, that's all." He took his time getting up. Tom came over and tried to help, but Julian waved him off. "Just a few hours of REM sleep and I'll be ready to roll."

"Okay," Tom said.

"Don't do anything great without me." Julian patted Tom's back and staggered down the hallway.

"I'll try not to," Tom called out as Julian worked his way toward the bedroom at the back of the cabin.

Halfway there, he stopped and took three deep breaths. He felt steadier.

He came to a door and entered a slightly musty room with a twin bed and a dresser. He struggled to open the window. When he finally did, a brisk breeze blew in. He connected his cell phone to his charger and fell onto the mattress. It was firm. His lower back ached. He pulled up a red comforter and shut his eyes . . .

He dreamed he was in a maze, running out of breath. He went down one row, turned right, then went down another. He stopped. Evelyn beckoned him. Then she pirouetted and summoned Richard. Julian stumbled off a cliff. His face burned. Julia yanked his leg. "Don't go." He fell into a stream. Rocks drubbed his head as Julia screamed. "Hold on. Please!" He landed in space, floating toward the sun, nothing to hold on to.

———

Julian opened his eyes. He was tangled in the comforter.

He freed himself and checked the bedside clock. It was 1 a.m. His mouth was dry.

He padded into the bathroom, splashed cold water on his face, and drank from the faucet. A phone rang. He plucked a towel off the rack and dried himself. Another ring—his cell phone. He hurried to answer it.

"Mr. Barnes," a woman whispered

"Yes."

"You've got to come now."

"Evelyn?" She sounded different.

"Alan found a cure. I told you he would."

Julia would live.

You go to jail.

He stood up straight, at attention. He figured he'd be doing plenty of that before long.

"I'll be right over." He turned on a lamp.

"We're at our place in Cairo." She gave him the address. He already had it. "We'll be waiting for you."

He hung up and buttoned his shirt as he left the bedroom. He paused at Tom's door. The bed was still made.

He checked the kitchen. Empty—just the refrigerator droning.

He went into Tom's office. The monitor's screen saver was on. A red hand splayed across it—five fingers spread out. A sticky note was on the desk beside the keyboard.

Went to see Slattery. T.

Maybe it was better this way. Tom didn't like this plan and might have tried to stop him. But Julian had only one option—just like Julia.

———

He followed a double yellow line, high beams on, his only guide in the pitch black ahead of and behind him. He turned on the radio. Alternative music, all electronic. He hadn't heard the song before but liked the beat. He usually preferred classical—mostly Mozart, whose short works had reminded him of a mishmash of mirth concocted from nursery rhymes when he was little. But there were times when he needed something raw. This was one of them.

He turned the volume higher. Bass thumped the speakers. The singer screamed, over and over, "It's not the same anymore."

He passed a restaurant on his left. It looked like a mansion, with white lights everywhere. People filed out. A man in a tuxedo held hands with a beautiful woman. She had dark hair and wore a strapless white gown. Reminded him of Julia. The couple walked toward a limousine. A bride and groom, about to begin their life together. Must be a great time.

The groom turned toward him. He looked like Richard.

"It's not the same anymore."

He punched a button on the radio. Silence.

The car's engine moaned as its tires hugged the pavement. He slowed for curves and deer crossings. He put on a news station. It was the top of the hour.

Red and orange lights flashed in his mirror. His stomach dropped a mile, but he maintained his speed. The police cruiser shifted into the left lane and passed him.

"More rain in the forecast, with hurricane winds . . ." The female voice on the radio was somber, like she'd let everyone down.

His cell rang. He rolled up the windows and pressed a button on his steering wheel.

"Mr. Barnes?" Evelyn's voice replaced the newscaster's on the car's speakers. "Are you on your way?"

He checked his GPS.

"Should be there in thirty minutes."

CHAPTER 33

*F*our fifty-six Bradford Avenue had two tall brick posts on either side of its entrance. The gate was open. The driveway was long, straight, and littered with potholes. Two-by-fours bridged a pair of orange drums off to the left. Julian slowed. The last two potholes were so wide he had no choice but to drive straight through, the car dipping.

He hit a paved patch and came to a castle. The door had a quarter-moon on it. To the left was an empty stone carport. He pulled into it.

Evelyn was on the top front step. Her blond hair was loose, down to her shoulders. She had on sneakers and a white terry-cloth robe.

"Sorry about the driveway," she said when he reached her. "We're in the midst of repaving it."

Their handshake felt inappropriate.

He headed inside. She was behind him.

The walls were paneled in mahogany. The lighting was soft. Looking up, he could see a floor above them that had a balcony lined with bookcases. There must have been thousands of hardcover books on the shelves.

"Alan's library?" Julian looked around.

"Those are mine." She extended her arm toward an open door. "Please wait in my study. I'll go get Alan."

Julian stepped into the room on his right. The ceiling light was on, one big incandescent ball. There were no windows. A hodgepodge of purple potpourri in glass jars was scattered about the room, which smelled of lavender. The walls were soft pink. A white leather couch was in front of an oak desk with nothing on top but a sleek laptop.

Evelyn and her brother entered. Wright wore a navy silk robe, initials in script on the breast pocket, matching pajamas, and clog slippers.

"I looked at the scans Rig sent," he said. "I got an idea. It actually came to me while taking a shower. That's happened before. I think it's the warm water. What do you think, Eve?"

She smiled. "I think you should tell Mr. Barnes your solution."

"I wouldn't remove the growth," he said. "I'd cut off its blood supply and it will shrink."

"You can actually do this?" Julian said.

"Absolutely. With a reduced caseload, I can control the symptoms of my disease, and I'll make sure I have my regular team assisting me. They're all top-notch."

"And what do you think of her prognosis overall?"

"Very good. The procedure is less invasive. The recovery time is faster, and as the tumor shrinks, she'll get relief from the headaches. That should come rather quickly."

"How long before it shrinks completely?" Julian imagined an orb of thick flesh nestled in Julia's head. Could a well-placed snip lead to its demise?

"I'd say about a year." Wright stroked his chin. "It should be completely benign by then, and Julia will be symptom-free."

"My brother is a genius." Evelyn looped her arm through Wright's. She was beaming. "It's not the first time he's accomplished such a feat."

"The tumor is in a precarious position," Wright said. "But I can reach the area I need to with a technique I've recently enhanced."

"Mr. Barnes," Evelyn said. "You have to tell them you're guilty."

"I remembered everything." His eyes were riveted on Wright. "You ran the light. You really don't remember?"

Wright held his stare. "It was green to me."

The telephone rang. Evelyn answered it.

"Hello? Yes. It's rather late . . . Oh. Hold on, I'll ask him." She placed the phone against her chest and turned to her brother. "It's Ben. He's nearby, says he has something important to discuss with us."

"Tell him to come over," Wright said. "Maybe he has good news."

"See you in a couple minutes." Evelyn hung up. "Mr. Barnes, we don't have much time. We need to free Alan so he can save Julia. You have to say you're guilty. That must be the plan."

The doorbell rang.

"That was quick." Evelyn gave Wright a strange look.

He shrugged.

"I'll get it," she said and scurried out of the room.

"I can save her," Wright said softly once they were alone.

"I know." Julian's pulsed raced. "But can you handle my going to prison in your place?"

"It won't be easy, but I'll take solace in knowing I saved a life that important to you."

Julian would, too.

"Mr. Barnes, I'm aware of what you're going to have to deal with." Wright looked sincere. "I will do everything I can to protect you from any harm while you're incarcerated."

Julian appreciated the sentiment but knew he'd be on his own. There was only so much anyone could do to keep him safe while he was locked up.

CHAPTER 34

Evelyn reentered the study with Tom and Slattery in tow. Slattery followed her over to Wright. Tom went to Julian, who was near the entrance.

"You're his brother?" Wright said to Tom.

"Proud to be." Tom put his arm around Julian and pulled him closer. "You okay?"

"Basically." Julian knew what he had to do. The hard part was doing it. "How did you find me?" he said under his breath.

"Homing device." Tom's mouth barely moved. "Same one we used to track Store. Figured you might take off without me."

"Your brother is going to confess." Evelyn stood in front of Wright. "Tell them, Mr. Barnes."

Tom walked up to her. "Before he lies," he said, "I think we should all hear the truth."

Evelyn and Julian glared at him.

"Call the police," Julian said. "I'm turning myself in."

Evelyn relaxed a bit.

"Detective Rollins is on his way." Slattery looked at his watch. "Probably be here in about twenty minutes. Enough time to answer some questions first."

"Which are?" Wright lifted an eyebrow.

"Initially"—Slattery removed his fedora—"the coroner's report had Cheryl's blood alcohol as negligible."

"That's not possible," Wright said. "Cheryl was . . . intoxicated. That's why I was taking her home."

Evelyn opened a desk drawer, took out a box of cigarettes, and lit one. She inhaled two quick puffs. Smoke surrounded her.

"John made a careless mistake," she said. "That's all. Let's not make a big deal about it. We have more pressing matters to contend with. Ben, as a longtime friend of the family, I would expect you to be cognizant of that fact." She batted the smoky air surrounding her with the back of her hand as if it had no right being there. "Besides, the omission was rectified in a revised report."

"That's true," Slattery said.

"So, Ben." Wright cleared his throat. "If the particular problem is solved, why does it need to be discussed, especially at this hour?"

"When I talked to John about the error," Slattery said, "he asked me if Evelyn was pissed. Needless to say, it was an awkward moment when John discovered I wasn't in on the plan."

"You're implying he and I were somehow in cahoots?" Evelyn laughed. "That's ridiculous."

"What plan?" Wright shifted his gaze between Slattery and Evelyn.

"Ms. Wright," Tom said, "you were at the party Cheryl attended the night she died?"

"Yes." Evelyn tightened the belt on her robe. "I have an office at Sunrise and often attend hospital functions."

"The foundation paid for the party," Slattery said.

"Marge was well-liked and had been with us awhile," Evelyn said. "I thought it was an appropriate gesture. This is a waste of time."

"Actually, she'd been there for less than a year," Slattery said. "Got that from Personnel. It was one of several interesting facts I garnered on my visit to Sunrise."

"Dr. Wright," Tom said, "you bought Cheryl an engagement ring?"

"Yes." He looked pained. "I was going to surprise her."

"You told your sister."

"Of course." Wright turned toward Slattery. "Ben, what's going on here?"

"John submitted a false coroner's report on Cheryl Star," Slattery said. "One that stated she died from the car accident."

"I don't understand." Wright narrowed his eyes. "She *did* die in the accident."

"She was already dead by then." Slattery gazed at the floor. "I'm sorry, Alan."

"Ben, what are you talking about?" Wright spread his arms.

"She was poisoned," Slattery said.

"Poisoned?" Wright wrinkled his face. "That's . . . You can't be serious."

"The only problem for Evelyn was that the original coroner's report included the correct blood alcohol level," Slattery said. "Cheryl wasn't drinking."

"She rarely drank." Wright stared into the middle distance. "I never thought to check John's report."

"You shouldn't have had to." Evelyn crossed her arms. "This is preposterous. I won't stand for these accusations in our household."

"I suspect Evelyn used the party as a ruse to drug Cheryl," Slattery said. "Evelyn must've cornered her at the bar, got her talking, and slipped something in her drink."

"That's crazy," Wright said. "Eve wouldn't . . . Do you have any proof, Ben?"

"I do." Slattery reached into his inside pocket and pulled out a document. "Apparently, Mr. McKenna didn't trust Evelyn, so he kept a copy of the *real* autopsy report in his electronic files, which Tom was able to access. That version says Cheryl died from an extremely poisonous species of gelsemium, her blood alcohol level was negligible, and none of her injuries from the accident were life-threatening." Slattery handed the report to Wright. "And she was ten weeks pregnant. Even if she'd been a drinker, she wouldn't have imbibed at the party."

Wright stared at the evidence while Evelyn looked on. After some time, the papers fell from his hands and fluttered to the floor.

Evelyn retrieved them.

"She was breathing when Angela buckled her in my vehicle." Wright looked dazed.

"I'm sure she was, Alan." Slattery put his hand on his shoulder. "But not for much longer. Lethal designer drugs initially induce grogginess, giving the killer time to transport their victims before they expire."

"I thought she was asleep." Wright briskly brushed away a tear. "That's all."

"Alan," Slattery said, "your sister had the foundation pay Melvin Winters to threaten killing Julia if Mr. Barnes remembered the accident."

Evelyn reached for her brother's hand. He wouldn't take it. She retied her robe.

"Mr. Winters had been at our house recently," Wright said. "I didn't know why."

"Ben." Evelyn gazed at Slattery. "How could you do this to us?"

"Evelyn, you know I don't take sides and always play fair." Slattery spun his hat in his hand. "If not for the accident, this would've been a murder investigation. Because once you showed up, Alan, Evelyn's plan went totally off the rails."

"What do you mean?" Wright looked stunned, disconnected.

"Evelyn was supposed to drive Cheryl home," Slattery said. "I bet she planned to put her to bed and hope everyone would assume Cheryl died of natural causes."

"Eve did insist on taking Cheryl home." Wright's voice was barely audible now. "I thought it odd at the time."

"The accident didn't kill Cheryl Star," Tom said. "You did, Evelyn."

Evelyn stepped backward.

"Eve . . . please," Wright said. "Tell me there's an explanation for all of this."

"Your sister loves you, Alan," Slattery said. "I always thought a little too much."

"I threw a party for an employee and now you think I'm a murderer?" Evelyn took a drag on her cigarette and watched the smoke stream from her mouth. "It's time for all of you to leave. We'll have to pick it up in the morning."

"This *is* the morning," Tom said. "Confess and let's get this over with, Eve."

"You never get to call me that!" Her voice was shrill as she jabbed her cigarette, now down to a butt, toward Wright. "Only Alan can call me that."

"Sorry," Tom said. "But the fact remains you killed Cheryl Star and paid your ex-lover to cover it up."

"You have no proof!"

"We have money transfers from Dr. Wright's foundation going to shell corporations set up for the coroner, John McKenna, and for Melvin Winters." Slattery reached into his opposite inside pocket and held a few folded papers toward Dr. Wright. "Here's some of the documentation."

"Where did you get—" Evelyn tried to snatch the papers, but her brother jerked them away and began reading them.

"Evelyn was the initiator and approver of the transactions in all instances," Slattery said.

"Eve." Wright looked tormented. "How . . . how could you?"

"Alan, can't you see?" Evelyn approached her brother. "We couldn't lose what we had."

Wright stepped backward, stumbled.

"Why would you want to spoil it?" Evelyn's mouth was crooked. "Don't lie and say you enjoyed being with her more than me. She wasn't your best friend. She certainly wasn't your soul mate."

"Eve . . ." Wright stared at his sister as if he'd never laid eyes on her. "What right . . . What on earth made you think—"

"It was so much better when we were children." Now Evelyn's voice was low. "'The best times of our lives,' you used to say. And after losing Mom and Dad, we still had each other."

"But—"

"I know you have needs I can't fulfill," Evelyn said. "There were plenty of women out there who were more than happy to do that. But Cheryl was different. I knew it right from the beginning. I could tell she wanted to settle down with you. I still gave her a chance, hoping we could come to some amicable arrangement. Her staying over on weekends—I could've compromised with that."

Julian couldn't figure out the expression on Wright's face. Was he dazed? Angry? Baffled? All three?

Wright heaved a deep sigh and looked into his sister's eyes. "If I've got this straight . . . you murdered the woman I loved—just so you and I would maintain our current living arrangement?"

"She tried to take you away from me." Evelyn's eyes were frantic. "She had to go. I had no choice. I'm not blaming you. Alan—please, you have to see it from my perspective."

The bell rang.

"That would be Detective Rollins," Slattery said. "I'll get it."

"And I'll keep an eye on *Evelyn*." Tom was shoulder to shoulder with her.

"I'm not running away," Evelyn said. "Shelia will fix this."

Slattery looked at Julian. "Let's take a walk."

He followed the investigator out of the room and toward the front door. Slattery opened it. A man in his forties with dark hair and a thick mustache stood there.

"Paul." Slattery shook his hand.

"She in there?" Rollins said.

"Her and her brother," Slattery said. "And Julian's kid brother, Tom, who I told you about."

"Nice to meet you in person, Julian," Rollins said. "We've already picked up Mr. Winters for questioning and arrested Mr. McKenna just as he was about to board a plane for Costa Rica. A productive night."

"We'll go greet the squad car at the foot of the driveway," Slattery said.

"Thanks," Rollins said. "Mike's always getting lost."

"I'm on it." Slattery donned his fedora.

Rollins went inside.

"You're an honest man, Slattery," Julian said. "I don't know much else about you, but I know that."

"Not much else you need to know." Slattery looked around and then reached into his overcoat. "You forgot this." He handed Julian a plastic bag.

It was the glass from Store's cabin.

CHAPTER 35

Julian was once again in a hospital waiting room with Ruth, Dina, and Reed, only this time it was Dr. Wright operating on Julia, and he wasn't removing the tumor but cutting off its life source. It seemed like a simple solution, one someone should have come up with sooner. But after Wright explained the intricacies, Julian realized why no one else had.

The procedure began at two. Wright sounded confident when he said it wouldn't take more than three hours. Still, since Evelyn's arrest he looked like he'd lost some of his swagger. She'd probably be sentenced to a mental institution for the rest of her life. Since none of the injuries anyone sustained in the accident were life threatening and Wright had made financial restitution, he was given a moving violation with four points added to his driver's license. All other charges against him were dropped. Melvin was out on bail, his case awaiting trial. McKenna took a plea bargain. His medical-examining days were over, and he'd spend five years in a state penitentiary for obstruction of justice.

At 5 p.m., Wright entered the waiting room and took off his mask.

"Everything went as planned," he said. "We'll continue to monitor the growth. The tumor should begin shrinking soon."

"Thank you, Doctor." Julian stuck out his hand. Wright shook it.

"Dr. Wright, you're a miracle worker." Ruth embraced him.

"You're all welcome." Wright hesitated, then turned and left.

———

"Can you forgive me?"

It was the following day. Julia lay in her hospital bed, its back at a forty-five degree angle. A bandage was around her head. Her lips were chapped, blue eyes still clear.

"I love you—more than ever," Julian said "That's the best I can say right now."

The sun shone bright. Outside, a man and a woman walked together holding hands. The woman rested her head on the man's shoulder as the couple disappeared into the distance.

"I miss you." Julia reached for him.

"I'm here."

"You know what I mean."

"I can't get the images of you two together out of my head." He held her hand. Her touch was everything he craved, yet he was still stuck.

"I'll wait for you." She squeezed his fingers. "Now that I have time."

———

"The tumor is still shrinking," Julia said. "Wright thinks in a year it'll disappear completely." They were on the phone. She was back living in her apartment. "I'm returning to work next week."

"I'll come by Tuesday and take you to lunch."

"Can we go to Manuel's?"

"Sounds good."

———

The next day Julian rang Ruth's doorbell.

"Thanks for making time for me. I just wanted to get my duffel bag and return these." Julian dropped her house keys into her hand. "I appreciate your trusting me with them." Should he have kept them longer? Another connection to Julia gone.

"It's you I have to thank." Ruth motioned for him to come in. "You were there for Julia when she needed you most." She patted his shoulder. "I'll always be grateful to you for that."

He nodded and bounded up the stairs. He entered the bedroom where he and Julia had stayed, keeping his eyes away from the bed as he barged into the bathroom. It was empty, wiped clean. A pine scent was in the air. Nothing of his anywhere in there. He imagined Julia looking into the mirror, brushing her hair as he kisses her shoulder and gives her butt a squeeze.

He shook off the image, strode back into the bedroom, and seized his bag off the closet shelf. He went back downstairs and into the living room. Ruth was by the fireplace.

"Julia has the same bag," she said.

"We got them before we met." He felt himself blush.

The doorbell rang. He looked at Ruth. She nodded.

"I might as well answer it." He went to the entrance and opened the door.

Julia was there. He gave her a hug and held up the bag in his hand.

"I just picked this up and wanted to return your mom's keys," he said.

"Oh." Julia's mouth formed a circle.

"I'd better get going." He felt powerless.

"Are we still on for lunch tomorrow?"

"Absolutely."

———

Julian hoisted the overnight bag onto the bed. He unzipped it—

Julia's black bikini bottom. The last time Julian had touched that, he was taking it off her. It was late in the afternoon, her skin warm from lying in the sun. They made love long and tenderly.

He moved the bathing suit aside. That's when he saw the corner of Julia's journal and realized he had the wrong bag.

Julia had taken a course called Clarifying Your Perspective Through Journaling. She'd once told him it helped her see things she wouldn't otherwise. He unzipped the bag and slipped out the spiral-bound notebook. It was hard-covered with a picture of a palm tree on it. It wasn't thick. He knew it could lie flat and had well-spaced lines—those were her requirements when they shopped for one together.

He opened the journal. A blank page. Julia said she always left one there. The next page had a date and words all over it. So did the next and the one after that. It was filled with words.

He slapped the book shut. He'd never seen the inside of one of her journals before.

The phone rang.

Could it be her? Some cosmic connection enabling her to tell when someone was about to violate her privacy?

The answering machine picked up. A hang-up.

He went to the kitchen table, sat, and opened the notebook once more. The night of the accident was the first entry.

CHAPTER 36

Julian's heart roared as perspiration pumped from his pores. Julia opened the door and stepped backward into the room. She was barefoot, wearing jeans and a red shirt.

He stepped inside and placed her luggage on the floor.

"I took your bag by mistake." He handed her her journal.

She turned crimson as she took the thin book.

"I saw there was an entry on the night of the accident." He pointed to the notebook now quaking in her hand.

"Did you read it?" She gave the impression that she wouldn't have minded if he had.

"I was going to." He took a deep breath. "Then I realized I needed to hear what happened from you."

"I agree. Would you like to sit?"

"Sure." He wedged himself in a corner of the couch.

She sat opposite him, feet tucked under her. "Richard had sent me a card on my last birthday," she said. "We hadn't seen each other since he left me. He said he wanted to get together. I never responded. He called the next week and asked me to dinner. I told him no."

Julian crossed his arms.

"The afternoon of the accident," she said, "Richard came into the bank." She peered at Julian. "We hadn't planned to meet."

He longed to reach out and touch her.

"He said he missed me and offered to buy me a drink—which I needed, after seeing him. And I admit, seeing him eat crow wasn't the worst thing for my ego. We went to McCann's and I downed two shots of vodka. They hit me harder than I expected. I got up, went to the ladies' room, and splashed cold water on my face. When I looked in the mirror, I asked myself, 'What am I doing?' My relationship with Richard had been so destructive. I thought maybe a part of me believed I didn't deserve happiness."

Julia's face was drawn, and shadows were under her eyes. She was beautiful.

"My mascara was running. A woman came in—she said I didn't look good. I told her what happened, that apparently I wasn't completely over Mr. Wrong and it kept me from having the relationship I wanted with Mr. Right, the man I loved."

"And?" He imagined her with some dark, intimidating woman.

"She said she'd had the same problem once. She took Mr. Wrong home, gave him great sex, then told him she never wanted to see him again. She said it was the most powerful moment in her life." Julia sighed. "It seemed like a good idea at the time."

"And you would've kept this from me?" It came out harsher than he intended.

"I hadn't thought it through like that."

"Fair enough." He loved her for who she was. Not who he thought she could be. "So . . . what happened next?"

"I told Richard to follow me to my apartment."

Julian winced.

"Richard could tell something was off. He tried to say something. I wouldn't let him. We went in separate cars and didn't say a word as we rode the elevator to my floor."

"That doesn't make it any easier for me," Julian said.

"I'm not trying to make things easier. I'm trying to tell you what happened—and what *didn't*."

He shook his head. "Go on."

"We sat in the living room. Richard kissed me and all I saw were your eyes, questioning me."

"That didn't stop you."

She looked down.

"Richard carried me into the bedroom, laid me on the bed, and started taking off my clothes. I said no, I'd do it, and—"

"Hold it." He closed his eyes for a moment before opening them again. "Okay. Go on."

"I got on top of him. I screamed an obscenity—I thought

that would help, but it didn't." She was standing in front of him. "I wasn't turned on. Richard wasn't either—he was barely inside me. That's when I realized I was the only one moving. I rolled off, looked at him, and knew he was dead." She sounded distant. "We didn't have great sex, Julian. We really didn't have any sex at all."

Remember—

He sees Julia's back—and that was all. Every other image he had visualized of what had happened, every awful fantasy of them together was wrong. Warmth radiated throughout his body.

"This changes things." He reached for her.

"It does?" She tilted her head. "I tried to tell you—"

"I know you did. It's not your fault."

"It really makes a difference?" She squinted.

"Yes, it does."

She stepped away from him. "There was a lot of grief between us." She shook her head slowly. "It seems strange. That this is the important part."

"I'm sorry . . . but it does make a difference." He approached her. "I couldn't have had sex with another woman while we were together. Our physical relationship is part of what I feel for you. Don't you see? I love you."

She fell into his arms and held him close. "I love you, Julian."

"I want to spend the rest of my life with you." He took in her scent and touched her cheek. He allowed himself to indulge.

"And I want to spend the rest of mine with you." She rested her forehead on his.

They kissed. It didn't take long before they undressed.

They made love, long and passionate. Afterward, they fell asleep. They woke up in each other's arms.

She was quiet, her body still.

"Is something bothering you?" he said.

"Julian, if he hadn't died, Richard and I would *really* have had sex. Terrible sex, but it would've happened. I don't want our whole relationship hinged on a simple twist of fate."

"I believe if he didn't die, something else would've prevented it. Maybe you wouldn't have gone through with it, or he would've realized it was a charade and stopped it. Who knows? Either way, it doesn't matter. What matters is that you and Richard weren't meant to be. It may have seemed like it at one time. But it isn't true. *We're* meant to be." He stuck himself with his thumb. "That's what I believe."

"We *are* meant to be together, hon." She held him closer. "But it won't always be easy, you know?"

"I do. But with you, it'll be worth it."

Her eyes went up and to the right. "And"—she smiled— "how about neither of us does any more betting on our destiny?" She had a hand on his chest.

"You make those kinds of wagers?" He shouldn't have been surprised. He smiled back.

"Probably a little too often. But I'm realizing it's a recipe for disaster in a serious relationship."

"Hey, lesson learned here. We need to commit to making

things work through our own efforts. Not on some games of chance."

"That's the only way we can be sure we'll always be together."

"I can't bear the thought of losing you." He kissed her. "No more bets with fate."

KEEP READING FOR A PREVIEW OF
THE NEW NOVEL FROM RICH SILVERS

SUM LIVES

Mark Holder is creating a battery that can get an SUV the equivalent of 640 mpg. If Mark is to succeed, he needs Eric Nolan's help. Both men are in love with Christy Sands—an extraordinarily beautiful and talented painter.

When Mark is suddenly confronted by businessmen who describe the economic destruction his invention would create, Mark must decide between his dream, his principles, and Christy's love.

CHAPTER 1

"There's always one," Cal said. "The one woman in your life you love more than any other. Then you tell yourself you've fallen in love again and eventually you get married, but deep down you know someone else owns your heart."

"Are you talking from firsthand experience?" Mark said.

"Me? Nah. I'm one of the lucky ones. I married her. I'd say that doesn't happen more than 20 percent of the time . . . and as I give it more thought, I'd say it's probably closer to 15."

"Now you have percentages?" Mark leaned against a warm concrete wall. His work boots were flat on the pavement and his knees were tented over half of a turkey hero lying on waxed paper that flapped in a September breeze. He and Cal were sitting on a paddleball court, having lunch. Cal had just turned thirty. But if Mark added up all his co-worker claimed to have done, Cal would be well north of sixty.

"Who's the love of your life?" Cal popped open his second energy drink.

"There's no one." Mark felt the spritz from Cal's can dry on his cheeks.

"You're thirty-two?" Cal had jet-black hair, a boyishly handsome face, and a short manicured beard. He was five-six but often seemed taller than that. He took a contemplative drag on his cigarette. Smoke shot out his mouth. "That's rare."

"What is?"

"Most have met her by your age."

Mark's hands were clenched. He breathed deep and let the oxygen out slowly. He did it again and his fingers relaxed.

"Well . . . I . . . haven't." He stared at the bright blue sky above the trees. "I love Colorado." He had lived in New York his entire life. "Look at that sky. Not a cloud as far as the eye can see." Mark had taken this job in construction to recharge himself. His real focus was his dream—he was creating a battery that would get an SUV the equivalent of 640 mpg. He had completed the first of four generations.

"You changing the subject?" Cal leaned back on his elbows.

"Well, I haven't met her yet."

"Dude, you probably know her."

"You say that based on what?" He didn't like being called *dude*.

"I observe." Cal flicked an ash off his cigarette. "I thought I made that clear?"

"Tell me more about living in Amsterdam." Mark threw a

rock. Leaves rustled and then a smack. He had quit smoking, but he could've used a cigarette then.

"Mind if I ask a couple of questions before we leave this topic?" If Cal were this relentless at work, Sully wouldn't ride him as much as he did.

"Ask away." Mark spread his arms.

"You ever tell a woman you love her?" Cal's fingertips shook, probably from copious amounts of caffeine. "I mean and *really* mean it."

"Twice."

Dana was funny and always there for him. But he was too young to get engaged. That's what she wanted and she couldn't understand why after two years he didn't feel the same.

"Quite often the first one is the one," Cal said.

"Not with me."

I gave you my heart and you broke it, she had said as she ran out the door. They never spoke after that.

"Who was the second?" Cal said.

"Christy."

Cal smiled, showing a lot of teeth.

"You were together for . . . ?" he said.

"Two years." He wouldn't reveal more than that.

"Four would've been better." Cal stroked his beard. "When was this?"

"Two years ago."

"Deuces wild." Cal looked at him from the corner of his eye. "You better act quickly."

"What are you talking about?" He gripped his thighs, suddenly sweating.

"Two years is long in the tooth to get back together after a breakup." Cal stabbed the air with the cigarette. "Granted, the time away from each other does some good, especially if there's a bad relationship or two in between, but I wouldn't wait much longer. The connection is fading."

"Christy is an extrovert. I'm not. It was at the heart of everything we fought about."

"You leave her?" Cal said.

"It was mutual."

Cal laughed like a hyena.

"What's so funny?"

"There's no Tooth Fairy, no Santa Claus, and no such thing as a mutual breakup." Cal took a sip from his can.

"So you're a relationship expert?"

"You'd be surprised what you learn when you pay attention."

"Christy left me. Is that what you want to hear?"

"Is it the truth?"

The truth was the last time he saw Christy she had just told him her best friend, Madeleine, was getting married and she was the maid of honor. She wanted him to go with her to the wedding. She promised to spend as much time with him as she could. But he knew Christy. She'd have a drink, start dancing, he'd get frustrated, and there could be a scene. Christy had said it would mean a lot to her if he came. *You'll have more fun without me,* he had said. That must've been when she had had enough.

"I have four categories—" Cal ticked off his fingers "—those who married their one true love, those who've lost her, those still looking for her—" holding his pinky "—and those who want to be alone." He peered at him. "There really are guys like that. But you're not one of them. I got a feeling Christy is your one true love." He stubbed out his cigarette. "In fact, I'd bet on it."

"You wouldn't say that if you knew anything about our relationship."

"She married?"

"Don't think so."

"Then you've still got a chance to get her back."

"Cal, you are so wrong about this." His stomach was on edge. He told himself to keep breathing. "She's not the one, definitely not. We're way too different."

"Different is good. How was the sex?"

"I'm not going there."

"You won't talk about it?" Cal snorted. "You know what that says?"

"I don't talk about the sex I've had with any woman." He crossed his arms and ankles.

"You need to loosen up."

"And you need to give up once in a while." Mark balled what was left of his lunch in the waxed paper and shoved the concoction into a brown paper bag. He got up off the ground feeling like a fool for thinking that he could give Cal some information and that he'd back off after that. That wasn't Cal. He just proved it—again.

"You don't like talking about yourself." Cal held out his hand.

"You're a genius." Mark pulled him up off the ground.

"Just know you've got someone to talk to." Cal crushed his can.

"Thanks."

"Guess we should head back." Cal looked distant. "Don't want to hear it from Sully."

They went through a gate and started the three-block walk back to the construction site.

"Christy's isn't the one." Mark experienced a jab of regret.

"I believe you," Cal said.

Cal didn't want to talk about this anymore? Mark should've been relieved but he wasn't. For the past two weeks he'd been imagining Christy in different places. He'd pass a café. She was seated in front of it. He was eating in his apartment and she was across from him at the dining room table. Yesterday, at the bank, the woman ahead of him on line had long red hair. He was sure it was Christy. He blinked. She turned around. She looked nothing like the woman he loved.

"You okay?" Cal asked when the construction site came into view.

"Never better." He wasn't as confident as he sounded.

"This can't be good." Cal pointed to their co-workers gathered in a tight cluster.

www.ingramcontent.com/pod-product-compliance
Lightning Source LLC
Chambersburg PA
CBHW021516240626
47154CB00002B/650